Lock Down Publications and Ca$h
Presents

PROBLEM SOLVED

Kill 'Em All

Written By
Christopher "Diesel" Hornezes

First Edition 2025

Printed in the United States of America

This is a work of fiction. Names, characters, places, and incidents either are products of the author's imagination or are used fictitiously. Any similarity to actual events or locales or persons, living or dead, is entirely coincidental.

Lock Down Publications
P.O. Box 944
Stockbridge, GA 30281
www.lockdownpublications.com

Like our page on Facebook: Lock Down Publications
www.facebook.com/lockdownpublications.ldp

By: Christopher A. Hornezes #704976
Racine Correctional Institution
P.O. Box 189
Phoenix, MD 21131

Stay Connected with Us!

Text **LOCKDOWN** to 22828 to stay up-to-date with new releases, sneak peaks, contests and more…

Like our page on Facebook:
Lock Down Publications

Join Lock Down Publications/The New Era Reading Group

Visit our website:
www.lockdownpublications.com

Follow us on Instagram:
Lock Down Publications

Email Us: We want to hear from you!

INTRODUCTION

Monique AKA Bunz leaned down on the Mahogany wood desk in Barry's luxurious office. she felt the 43-year-old Italian sliding his hard dick into her asshole, as she held her cheeks open for him. She felt the tip enter her and winced from the slight pain stretching her out, but she didn't stop him. Fulfilling all his sexual desires had been key to get her to this point. She was on a mission, and was not leaving without making it happen.

Barry clenched his teeth as the warmth of her enveloped his throbbing cock. He grunted and cursed, loving how such a beautiful woman with such a fat round ass let him do whatever he wanted to her. He'd always had a fetish for thick Black women, like most men, so when he found her shaking her ass for chump change in a club, he *had* to get her.

"Ooohh *yeeeaaah!*" he groaned, holding onto her wide hips, as he thrust in and out of her. "You like that, Bunz? Huh? Tell me you like how my cock feels in your ass!"

"Mmmmm, I *love* it, Barry!" she capped, ready for him to bust his nut. Then he could go do what he always did after she let him fuck her in her ass, and she could make the move she'd been planning for the last two years happen.

"Fuck my ass, baby! Fuck my ass like it's *all* yours, and only yours!"

She put on a show for him, faking her pleasure, hyping his head up to make him feel like he was the man. Barry reached out and grabbed her silky long brown hair and wrapped it around his hand. He gave her all that he had, which had no real effect on her. In minutes, he started grunting and cursing, feeling his nut rising. His eyes rolled to the back of his head as he groaned gutturally.

Bunz could tell he was getting close. She could feel his dick spasming inside of her ass so she reached her right hand back and pulled his dick out of her. Barry stroked his cock while she held her juicy 46-inch ass open for him.

Seconds later, he came. He roared animalistically as he skeeted globs of hot cum all over her asshole. Barry howled as he emptied himself. Bunz felt all the hot droplets splattering in her crevice, filling it up. Once he was done, she waited, knowing the last thing he loved to do after he busted his nut, was coming.

Barry dropped down to his knees and fulfilled his sick-ass fantasy; he started slurping up his own cum out of her crack. He licked her clean and swallowed every last drop. Curling her lip up in disgust, Bunz continued to act like it was a turn on for her, even if the shit was nasty. Barry had *long* money, and money was her motive.

"God, I love this great big ass! It really reminds me of glazed Honey Buns! That's how you got your name, isn't it, Shannell?" he asked, calling her by what she had *told* him was her government name.

"Uh huh," she said, hiding her smirk, detesting the lame-ass dude with a passion.

Barry smacked her ass and kneaded it like it was cookie dough. He was infatuated with the size and shape of it. Bunz giggled and raised herself up from his desk. Turning to him, she smiled up at him, looking him in his eyes, seeing the sparkle inside of his.

"I think we should get back to your party now, Barry. Your wife and daughter are probably wondering where Daddy Dearest has gone. What do you think they'll do if they find out that your so-called '*business partner*' is really your whore?"

Barry waved that off. "*I* run this house, Shannell. Me. When I'm with you, I don't give a fuck about anyone else. Let me go use the bathroom really fast," he told her, then he hurried off towards where the private bathroom in his of the grand 20,000-square-foot Victorian mansion he owned. Slipping inside, Barry shut the door and locked it.

Bunz counted down from five, then she hopped to it. It was the moment she had been waiting for to come, for *so* long. She hurried to pull her silk panties and black pantyhose up from around her ankles. She fixed the little red wool skirt that went with the red business suit that made her look worthy of standing next to Kamala Harris.

Listening, she could hear Barry snorting inside of the bathroom. She knew he was *powdering* his nose as usual. He was a certified cokehead so she knew she had at *least* 7 minutes before he came out.

Okay! Here we go! she thought to herself, nervous as hell, but ready to make everything she'd done with the old bastard for the last two years well worth the embarrassment.

Over in the corner of Barry's office, a Picasso was hung on the wall. Bunz quick-stepped over to it and gently lifted it off the hook. She set it down on the suede button-tuck couch that it'd been hanging over, then looked back at the bathroom once more. She could still hear snorting, followed by grunting and groaning. After a second of silence, she heard a sneeze, then a curse before more snorting started up.

Turning back to the wall, an old school safe with a combination lock was hidden behind where the painting had been. Bunz had seen him enter the combination so many times that she could recite it in her sleep, but she had never been left alone in his office. She hurried to enter the combination, turning the dial to each number. Just under ten seconds later, the safe was unlocked. *YES!* she screamed inside, as she was just moments away from *the* biggest score ever.

Opening the safe, she saw it, around the neck of a plastic manikin inside, gleaming brightly, even in a dark space. She gasped in awe of the big vintage white-gold necklace, embedded with flawless VVS diamonds. They hypnotized her with their glimmering shine. Bunz was so entranced by the priceless jewelry that she had stopped paying attention to anything else.

"Well, well, well, what a surprise."

Bunz shrieked when she heard Barry's voice behind her. She spun around and saw him, just a few feet away. In his hand was a 9- millimeter Sig Sauer. Bunz looked at the gun then at him.

"Going to try and steal from me?" he said to her, taking a step in her direction. "I *knew* you were a thieving little slut! You've been sucking and fucking me for the last two years; you left your boyfriend to come be my bitch!"

Bunz remained silent as he closed the gap between them. She refused to show fear to a white man. Barry backed her up against the wall behind her. Bunz stared into his eyes defiantly, mentally challenging his gangster, which pissed him off even more.

"Open your mouth, you thieving little whore! Now!" he demanded.

She continued to stare at him with pure malice in her eyes.

WHAM!

He struck her in the head with his cannon. Bunz yelped out in pain as the blow rattled her.

"Open your fucking mouth, bitch!"

She obeyed and he forced the barrel of his gun into her mouth.

"Now suck my gun the way you suck my cock, bitch! Make it cum *real* hard, all down your throat!"

Bunz did as she was told. She started sucking on the barrel. Tears of hatred fell from her eyes as he made her feel lower than dirt. She hated the fact that in an instant, he could pull the trigger, and it was over. Just then, a knock came at the door. Barry quickly pulled his gun out of Bunz's mouth and yelled out, *"Who is it?"*

"It's me, Barry! What are you doing in there? Everyone's looking for you!" he heard his wife holler from the other side.

Angrily, Barry turned and faced the door and shouted back. *"I'm on a business call, Irene! Just go back to the party and I'll be back in a minute!"*

"Well hurry up. Your mother's getting on my goddamn nerves!" Irene yelled back, then she left.

Barry muttered a curse under his breath, shaking his head. "A'right, you little cum-swallowing whore," he said, turning back to finish. "Where were we?"

Bunz stood there, hands behind her back and a smirk on her face. "You were about to die, you punk ass, bitch ass cracker," she said, then pulled her right hand from behind her back.

Barry saw an ice pick in her hand and gasped as she lunged at him. He tried to raise and point his gun to pop her ass, but she was faster.

"Aaaaahhhhh fuck!"

He howled in pain when Bunz stabbed him right in his left eye with the pic. The explosive pain made him drop the gun. He struggled to see and grab the pic before he could manage to wrap his hand around it. He yanked it out and blood started pouring from the hole left in his face.

"You bitch," he yelled. *"You're gonna die for this shit!"*

"Not before you do, *pussy,"* Barry heard her say.

He quickly turned in the direction he'd heard her voice. With his good eye, he saw her, just feet away, she had his gun, pointed right at him.

"So long, Barry," she said, then she pulled the trigger.

BOC! BOC! BOC! BOC! BOC! BOC! BOC! BOC!

Bunz shot him repeatedly, hitting him in his chest, throat, and his face. Barry was dead before he even hit the floor. For a minute, she just stared down at the dead billionaire. Blood poured through the bullet holes, pooling around him. After months of sucking his dick, letting him fuck her in every hole, and preform some vile sex acts on her, he was dead, and she was about to come up.

"Bitch ass nigga," she said to the dead man at her feet.

Tucking the gun into the rear waistline of her skirt, she got the necklace out of the safe, and stuffed it down her skirt, into her pantyhose. She was about to close the door, when she noticed a small barely noticeable compartment inside of the safe. She reached in a pressed on it, making it pop open, revealing a little suede bag that was the size of a Crown Royal bag.

She grabbed it, untied the gold strings, and looked inside.

"Oh shit!" she gasped, seeing little plastic bags with pink, purple, and blue baby diamonds in them. "Holy *shit*! This spaghetti eatin' creep was holdin' for real!"

BAM! BAM! BAM!

"*Barry!*"

Bunz heard his wife's voice from outside the office and knew it was time to go. Just as she tucked the bag of colorful stones into her pantyhose with the necklace, she heard the unmistakable sound of a key being inserted into the lock and the door being unlocked…

***

The big armed bodyguard ran into the office, with his semi-automatic Glock drawn. The gunshots that had come from inside had gotten Irene's attention and she'd called her and her husband's main security and ran to the office to see what the hell was going on.

"Shit!" the guard cursed when he saw Barry on the floor, surrounded by blood and missing an eye.

"*Barry! Oh my God!*" Irene cried out when she saw him.

The young blonde ran to him and dropped to her knees, screaming and crying. She cradled him, pleading for him to wake up. Without him, her world would crumble. He had never let her into the billion-dollar diamond dealing empire he had single-handedly built, so she and their 18-year-old daughter were shit out of luck.

The guard ran around the office, frantically searching for whoever shot and killed his boss. He ran to the big window that opened to a balcony, peering over, looking out into the darkness of the expansive backyard and saw… nothing.

Running back in, he looked around, but there was no sign of anyone else.

"Ma'am, whoever did this got away," he said, and unhooked his 2-way radio from his belt to radio for his crew to call the cops.

Sobbing over her dead husband, Irene happened to look up right as the door to the office started to move. When she saw a woman in a red skirt suit step out from behind it, and point a gun at the bodyguard's head, she screamed.

BOC!

***

Bunz put one in the back of the bodyguard's dome, pushing his brains out through a gaping hole in the center of his forehead. The big man fell forward, crashing to the floor like a big oak tree being cut down, landing inches away from where Irene and her dead husband were.

Irene looked up at the beautiful woman. "Why?" she cried.

Bunz pointed the gun right at Irene's face.

BOC!

She shot her in her right eye, killing her instantly.

"I'm a bad bitch that just got super rich," Bunz said to the dead woman.

With the diamonds tucked away and no one to point the finger at her, she ran to the balcony window, and climbed out, dropping to the ground like a skilled cat burglar, then she high tailed it out of there, with millions of dollars' worth of rare precious stones stashed in her pantyhose.

***

Once Bunz was finally out of the estate, she made her way to the '99 Mercedes E500 that she had left waiting around the corner. Behind her was nothing but chaos and it made her smile. She almost wanted to wait and see what they would do next but now was not the time. There were cops everywhere and it was time to get the fuck out of "Paradise".

Chapter 1

With no intention on stopping until she was out of California, Bunz made it down to I-80 and headed east towards Nevada. Adrenaline, anger, and fear of getting caught before she could make it back to the home she'd been dying to get back to for so long, fueled her to keep going.

Half past midnight, her body relaxed a little as she crossed into Nevada. She saw signs for Reno and finally exhaustion hit. The events of the day had finally caught up with her and she needed to sleep. Not for a full eight hours. No, just long enough to get a little pep and get back on the road. But she also needed to stop somewhere that would take cash, less chance of getting caught that way.

As she drove, looking for somewhere to rest she saw *him*. She missed him so damn much it made her chest hurt. But what hurt even more was knowing that he probably had someone new in her spot. Even that knowledge wasn't enough to keep her from going home to him.

Even though she had done him wrong after everything he had done for her, she'd truly loved him, and she still needed him. Now that she had finished the game, she was playing the only place she wanted to be was laid up with him. A little sliver of hope popped up in her chest. Maybe, just maybe when he saw what she had done, what she had gotten for *them* he would forgive her. And then she could spend the rest of their lives making up for her fuck ups to him.

***

Bunz was 25 and just knew she was *her.* Being mixed with Jamaican, Puerto Rican, and Cambodian had afforded her the kind of beauty that most women tried to buy. She was what many called exotic and the fact that she was naturally what other women wanted to be made them hate, *hard.*

She was a dime. Period. Standing 5'8, blessed with 36-DD cup breasts, a 26-inch waist, and a *GOOD-GOD-ALMIGHTY* fat ass, Bunz made heads turn everywhere she went. Her flawless skin was the color of delicious caramel. Her naturally long hair reached down to her ass. She was every bit a baddie and she knew it too.

Life had made her tough because otherwise the streets would have eaten her up. They almost did anyways. At 8 her parents had decided drugs were far more important than an extra mouth to feed and had sent her off with sex traffickers. 2 years of torture later she ran from her own little slice of hell only to be caught up and sent somewhere that was somehow worse.

The place that was supposed to be her haven brought her to yet another pervert that was attracted to her young body. After all, if she had the nerve to stay in his house rent free then she could give something up. Or at least that was what he told her. And so, she ran... again, running until she couldn't run anymore. She was terrified of nearly everyone she encountered, beaten down physically and mentally.

Her luck changed, though, when she met a loving lesbian couple from Jacksonville. The two took her into their lavish home and finally showed her *real* love and *real* affection. She lived in a big house, had designer clothes, and was put in the best schools, but that wasn't meant to last.

And one day after she had finally let her guard down the only real parents she'd ever had were gunned down in their own homes. All the beauty she had grown used to had come from drug money. Her *moms* had gotten caught with enough dope to fund them for years by the feds. Instead of going down alone they started working with them and that cost them their lives, and hers too.

At 15 she escaped and fled certain death. With no real options she turned to selling her body at truck stops so she could get as far away from Florida as possible. It took damn near a full year before she was able to hop on a Greyhound and made her way to Chicago, settling out west in a neighborhood known as K-Town. Out in Chiraq, Bunz continued selling pussy to men that cared more about how she *looked* grown but wasn't. Turned out a lot of ballers had a thing for someone young with her skills, so she got her money up quick.

Once she turned 18, she was finally able to get into clubs and got a spot as a dancer for a very popular in a south Chicago suburb. She shook ass for cash and fucked for a buck until she was 21. On her 21st birthday she met a man that stole her breath away, when he came in to celebrate his own 21st b-day, with a few of his friends.

He had her smitten without ever having spoken a word to her. A few of the other dancers jumped on him and his guys, giving lap dances, getting big faces rained on them. But when Bunz made her presence known, all eyes were on her, as usual.

That night started something real between the two of them. He was a dope boy who was making real moves in the streets of Chicago. He was like something she had never seen before, and she loved that she was his and he was hers. It was damn near perfect.

Even with this new look she continued dancing, despite knowing he wanted her to quit. As much as he wanted it, he never pressured her into it. After all, he had met her in the strip club, and he had never been insecure. As long as she understood that she was with him, and they were making moves together he was good.

But as Bunz had learned every sunny day had to end and that end came when there was a party like none other being thrown in her club. Men and women with the kind of money she had only ever dreamed of touching were everywhere and one of them noticed her. An Italian mobster who sold diamonds wanted *her.*

He asked her out, and Bunz found herself saying '*yes*', despite that she had a man at home. He took her out to the most expensive restaurants, took her shopping at top-of-the-line clothing boutiques, and cashed out on her daily. Riding around with him as he went to meetings around Chicago, chauffeured in foreign automobiles, and driving exotic cars, had Bunz nearly forgetting about her man. The money had her hooked. She couldn't see past it.

So, when the day came, and he asked her to move to California with him she said yes. She was shocked by how quick her answer came but how could it not. Money was the motive, and this was no different to her. So, she packed her bags and dipped in the middle of the night leaving behind a man she loved for Paradise.

But Paradise wasn't anything like its name. Bunz became his sex slave and it kept her seeing so many big faces, driving his cars, wearing the best designer labels on the market. She felt regret at the loss of a real love but for her new position as Barry Paulmatti's bitch she could live with that regret. Or at least she thought she could, until she discovered his secret. *A wife and daughter.*

Hurt wasn't the word for what she felt. She couldn't believe she never knew he was married. But the signs had always been there. He hadn't moved her into his house but had given her something small nearby. He had never stayed the night, and he called her, but she had never even had a number to call him at. She was pussy, plain and simple. And that realization made her vengeful and she started plotting on him, wanting to hit him where it hurt, in his pockets.

Barry was the definition of a pillow talker. After a few drinks he just couldn't keep his mouth shut. One night at a gentlemen's club he told her all about a rare necklace worth millions that he just so happened to have in his safe. He didn't slip up enough to tell her where but that was enough for a plan to form.

It took Bunz nearly a year to discover where he kept it. She knew she had to get into his house and the answer to that was simple. Pussy. Good pussy had power, and she knew her shit was good. Once they started fucking in his house it was *always* in his office. Finally, after months of that shit he started to get comfortable with her around, taking the Picasso off the wall and entering the code like she would never be crazy enough to try him. After three different times, she memorized the combination and started planning to get back to Illinois with the necklace. As much as she hated Barry and the things he made her do, she refused to leave without it.

Two years of creeping around and fulfilling sexual fantasies that would make even the freakiest niggas sick and Bunz had finally made her move and had put Barry, the Diamond Man down, making off with more than a two million dollars' worth of diamonds.

***

Breezing through the desert, Bunz continued to push herself along the desolate highway until she saw signs on the side for a few restaurants, gas stations, truck stops, and motels. She took the first exit that came up and went to a Motel 6. After she got the room with cash and no ID, she let out a small sigh of relief and ran back to her parked car to grab everything she needed. She could finally breathe.

Once in the room she made a beeline for the shower. She needed everything from the past two years off. Under the hot water it felt like she could wash her sins away. Barry, gone, sweat, gone, blood and grime, gone. As she cleansed herself her mind followed, and she burst into tears. She hadn't cried in a long ass time but as everything came flooding back, she just couldn't help it. The water ran cold before she finally got out and wrapped a dry, uncomfortable towel around her body. And before she knew it, she was asleep.

Hours later she got up feeling like a brand-new person. To compliment the feeling, she put on a sleeveless belly top, a leather mini skirt, and 6=inch stiletto pumps. She threw her hair up in a bun and grabbed all her bags. She needed to make it to Utah or Colorado before sunset and she wasn't stopping till she was there.

***

Shit! she thought to herself, when she stepped out of the room and saw a dark blue Ford Explorer with *Reno PD* on the side of it. Behind the wheel, she could see a heavy-set white guy, with coke-bottle glasses, and freckles. It was too late to turn back because he had damn sure seen her.

"Hey, there, ma'am! You happen to see who got outta this Mercedes?" the cop asked her.

Shocked that he didn't automatically assume that she was the driver, Bunz looked to her right, just as the door to another room opened, and two scantily clad prostitutes exited, with a young white guy in a business suit.

"Them!" Bunz pointed at the trio without a moment of hesitation.

The three heard Bunz shout and looked at her before they saw the cop. The two whores and their john cursed.

"*Misty! Trixie! Get your asses over here,*" the cop yelled to them, obviously aware of who the ladies were.

The two prostitutes took off running in one direction, while the guy ran in another. The cop slammed his vehicle into reverse and shot backwards to catch the girls. Bunz muttered a curse under her breath. There was no way she could jump back in this car, it was hot. There was only one other choice. She scooped up her bags and made her way to the lobby, she was gonna have to hop on a Greyhound.

***

Inside, she felt instant relief from the sweltering heat but wasted no time basking in the cool air. She went to where a wall had a bunch of postings, looking for a way out of the area, before cops came deep to find the real driver of the car. And since she had pointed them in the wrong direction she would be their first stop.

"Hey, chula?"

Bunz heard a man's voice behind her. She turned around and saw a tall Hispanic man with dark brown skin, graying hair, and a thick mustache a few feet away from her. He was dressed in a polo shirt with Ernie's Auto Sales on the chest, jeans and cowboy boots. His belt had a big silver Ford belt buckle.

"You look lost. Can I assist you with a ride somewhere?" the guy asked her.

"I'm looking to get a taxi or to get a Greyhound. Can you take me to wherever I can get either one?" Bunz asked him.

"Sure. I actually own a car dealership a few miles away from here, and there happens to be a bus depot across from my lot. If you're ready, we can go now."

"Yes. Please and thank you...um...?"

"Oh. Please excuse me. My name's Ernie Castañeda. And you are?"

"Charlotte Bingham," she lied. "Nice to meet you, Ernie. Can we go?"

"Sure. Vamos," Ernie told her, giving her a warm smile, then like a gentleman, he grabbed her bags and helped her out to where his older Jeep Wrangler sat parked.

***

A few miles from the Motel 6, Ernie pointed her to what had to have been an old shopping plaza. There were no stores but there was a Greyhound station. *Thank God.*

"A bus actually just left before I left my lot," he told her as he continued driving. "It's gonna' be a while before the next one, so if you want, you can come to my business and get something to eat and drink?"

Bunz sighed and nodded. She was so ready to get the fuck out of the west, but with no phone, no car, and only $5,000 in cash, she really had no choice. Ernie reached his used car dealership and turned in. No other salespeople nor car buyers were there yet. It was still very early in the morning.

Bunz saw a variety of cars that had very low prices. She saw an older 1998 Chevy Malibu with a sales sticker displaying *$1,350* for the price. That would be perfect. Then she would still have cash and wouldn't have to keep stopping at bus stops.

"What's up with the Malibu, Ernie?" she asked, as he parked at his office.

Cutting the engine off, Ernie looked at her. "You like it?"

She nodded. "I can afford it. Maybe I could just buy it and drive home. My parents would be happy to see that I have a car." It was a lie but it was better than anything else she could've come up with.

Ernie chuckled. "Well, how about we go inside my office and see about getting the price a little lower for the beautiful lady, eh?"

"Uh….sure," Bunz replied, seeing a shit-eating grin growing on his face.

Chapter 2

Carrying her bag, Ernie led her into the dealership building, back to where his dusty office was. He set her bag down next to the door, waited until she stepped in and then shut the door… and locked it.

"Okay, you want the Malibu. I want $1,350 for it," he told her, stepping close to her, "but, depending on how *bad* you want it…I might be willing to let it go for just a few hundred."

Bunz looked at the man and saw him lick his lips.

"How 'bout it, chula?" he asked. "I take care of you…you take care of me, you get your car, and we can both be happy."

She looked down and saw his dick pressing out from the crotch of his jeans. She sighed, before dropping to her knees. Working quickly, she undid his pants and freed his dick before he pushed into her mouth. The smell that came from his dick was foul and she had to fight the urge to pull back. She had to make shit happen. So, like all the times before she hardened her heart and went somewhere else in her mind.

"Ooohhh, *yeah*! Wooo! Yeah, chula!" he groaned as she sucked his cock, using one hand to jerk his shaft. "I knew you could suck a good dick when I saw you! Oh, this feels so good!"

He grabbed her head and started fucking her face, making her gag by ramming his dick down her throat. Bunz closed her eyes and made herself think about five minutes from that moment. She'd have a car and wouldn't have to worry about a bus, taxi, or hell even the cops looking for a stolen car. Ernie cursed, pumping himself in and out of her mouth. Less than a minute later he was pulling himself out of her mouth and slapping it on her face like a fucking porno. He grabbed her under her arm and pushed her towards his desk, forcing her to bend over.

"Dios mio, chula, what a fat juicy ass you have," he told her as he raised her little skirt up.

SMACK!

His hand connected to her ass... hard. Causing her to shriek she but took it. Ernie grabbed her butt cheeks and spread them apart. He spit a wad of saliva down into her crack and rubbed his cock in it, lubing her asshole up. She clenched her teeth, knowing what was to come.

He entered her asshole hard and fast and she cried out in pain, but it didn't make him stop. He brutally ass-fucked her until he felt his nut rising. Pulling his dick out, Ernie gripped it and jerked, busting his nut all over her ass, emptying himself.

"WOOO! FUCK!" he hollered out.

"Happy now?" Bunz asked, with a sore asshole.

"Hmmmm..." Ernie pulled his pants back up and fixed his belt, as she turned around and started fixing her own clothes. "I'll be happy when you let me get those diamonds you stole from the diamond man, chula."

Bunz gasped in shock and tried to run. Before she could get too far his hands were around her throat and she was pinned to the desk.

"Where are they, puta?! Give 'em up and I won't hurt you! If you don't then I'm gonna fuck your ass with a tire iron until you cough 'em up!"

"I... d-don't....kn-kn-know!" she managed to get out with his hand cutting off her air.

Ernie put his other hand around her neck and started squeezing harder making her panic. She fought to get his hands off her, but it was useless.

"I know you're the one that killed him, his *pinche* whore wife, and the bodyguard, bitch! You match the description his people put out on you! It's not gonna be the cops you gotta worry about, though, Barry was a mobster! A *made* man! You're gonna die, you stupid bitch! *Give me the diamonds bitch!*"

He didn't even pause long enough to let her answer before he lifted a hand and smacked the shit out of her. If she didn't know any better, she would think he had hit her with a fucking brick. Her cries seemed to fuel him as he let her go and started beating her ass like she was a man or something. He didn't even stop when the pain made her piss herself.

This motherfucker's trying to kill me, she thought to herself, balling up as Ernie kicked and stomped her. He laughed as he continued to assault her like it was nothing.

"You know what? They must be in your bag," he said finally remembering that that was all she had with her, "Let's go have a look, eh?"

As he turned to go check her bags, Bunz was suddenly hit with a rage that made her blood boil. In an instant, all the horrible things men had done to her over the years she'd spent being Barry's bitch had rushed back to her. It was like the beating never happened as she jumped up from the floor and flew into a frenzied state. Ernie had just got to her bags when he heard her scream. He turned around and saw her running towards him.

"Shit!" he yelled when she dove on him.

Bunz took him to the ground and started fighting him just like he had done to her. She hit him in his face hard and fast over and over. There wasn't a moment for him to catch his breath and he knew he had underestimated her. He tried to push her off him, but Bunz wasn't going for any of that shit. Instead of releasing him, she dropped her face down to his and bit down as hard as she could around his nose.

"Aaagh! Fuck! Stooop! Stooop!" Ernie screamed as she bit down as hard as she could, breaking through the skin.

22

He screamed in agony while she yanked and pulled like a dog with a bone. Finally, his nose ripped away from his face and blood went everywhere. Somehow that still wasn't enough for her. She bit down on his exposed Adam's Apple with every bit of strength left in her body and pulled, ripping his throat out.

The sounds of him dying snapped Bunz out of her rage induced fight and she spit the part of his Adam's apple that was still in her mouth out. But she didn't move as she watched him take his last breath.

"What the fuck?" she said to herself, tripping that she now had *four* bodies, in a little under 24 hours, millions of dollars' worth of hot rocks, and people looking for her.

With no time to stick around, Bunz looked around, trying to figure out what the hell to do. When she thought about what *he* would do in a situation like this, she ran around to look for anything flammable.

In a metal cabinet by Ernie's desk, she found cleaning supplies and a can of gasoline. She took them all out and set them on the desk. Before she started dousing the place, she scrambled around to find the keys to any vehicle she could.

She found racks of them in a metal lock box mounted to the wall in his office. Opening it, she grabbed the first set of keys she laid eyes one. Something Ford, she wasn't sure, but it had a key and a key fob and that was all she knew. Moving quickly, she searched for a minute before she found the temporary plates and shoved all the items in her bag. Finally, she started dousing the office in everything she had found.

She made sure to cover Ernie's body in the gas and went from there. Bunz grabbed her bag and rushed out of the office. In the front lobby area, she started searching for something, anything that would actually start a fire. Opening a desk drawer, she found a lighter and a newspaper. She lit it and dropped it into the office where the body still was.

Flames instantly came to life and turned the office into an inferno. Right as she was running out, she grabbed a pair of dark shades and a mesh trucker hat from off another metal filing cabinet, then hauled ass out of the building. She was beyond relieved to see that there was still nobody on the property yet.

Holding the alarm fob up, Bunz pressed the button. She heard beeping come from the other side of the lot. She ran as fast as she could in her high-heels, as the building began burning brightly, to where a dark red 2001 Ford F-150 sat.

She tossed her bag in and hopped in behind the wheel. Starting the engine, she shrieked excitedly to see that it had a full tank of gas. Bunz slammed it into drive, mashed the gas, and peeled out of the lot, just as the entire dealership building became a ball of fire.

***

After 24 hours of nonstop driving Bunz crossed the Mississippi River from Iowa into Illinois. She was finally home, and it showed in the way that she easily navigated the streets. She continued east on the I-88 to Chicago.

Once she got into Chicago's city limits, Bunz felt way safer than she had since she had started her drive. She even turned the music on, realizing that she hadn't heard a single song the whole 1,940-mile trip. Tee Grizzley's new *IDGAF* featuring Mariah the Scientist and Chris Brown played from Chicago's 107.5 WGCI radio station. Bunz continued cruising north up the Dan Ryan Expressway, merging off when the Edens came up.

Almost another hour later, in Gurnee, she was passing by a Cracker Barrel there, an IHOP, and a Joe's Crab Shack as her stomach rumbled in hunger. She got off at the exit and went to the least busy IHOP, parking her steamer all the way in the back of the lot.

She dug in her duffle bag grabbing her money and the diamonds, shoving it all in her pocket to make sure that even if the car was stolen, she'd have what she'd worked hard for.

Now was the time for a well-deserved meal and a break from being behind the wheel.

***

After she'd gorged herself on the delicious apple cinnamon-topped pancakes, bacon, and scrambled eggs she'd ordered, she dropped a nice tip on the table and made her way back to her car. Hopping back into the F-150, Bunz got back onto Grand, and headed east, rolling through Gurnee, towards Waukegan. Barely anyone was out with it being so late in the night, so it took less than twenty minutes for her to reach Wauk-Town, as those that grew up in the suburban town called it. She was surprised to see that not much had changed since she left in 2022. Other than a few new stores, it all still looked the same to her.

Bunz drove all the way down to Grand and Lewis Avenue and made a right turn where she entered a residential area with modest 2-level homes with driveways, front and backyards lining both sides of the street. She passed by six houses and came up to the driveway of a home with a brick facade, white siding, with a tall tree in the front yard.

Bunz took a deep breath to try steeling her nerves that were going haywire. She was moments away from seeing his face. What scared the shit out of her, was *how* his face would look like when she showed up unannounced.

***

She turned into the driveway and rolled past the house's side door entrance. In the rear was a 2-car garage; she got to the back of the house and hooked a tight left turn onto a square concrete parking pad there, and parked, killing the engine.

For a minute, Bunz sat there, terrified with worry. She couldn't believe that she'd made it back. Tears began filling her eyes as she again had flashbacks of all the things that had nearly taken her life while she was putting her master plan to action. She thought about the thing that *she* had done to people, and the things that people had done to *her*.

Her thoughts were abruptly interrupted when tapping on her window came out of nowhere. Bunz turned to her left and found herself staring down the business end of a sawed-off shotgun.

Chapter 3

"Noo! Don't shoot, it's me, Eric!" she screamed out of her window.

Eric lowered the gun when he heard her voice, and she could see nothing but pure shock on his face.

"Monique?" he asked, with a bewildered expression etched in his face.

Opening her door, Bunz's 6'1" ex-boyfriend, stood with two bulky XXL Bullies, both dark-brown brindle, with clipped ears, making them look like the vicious beasts that they were.

"Yeah, E. It's me… I'm… home," Bunz said, so nervous that she felt like she might pee on herself from the look in his eyes.

Eric was rendered speechless as he stared at the woman who had just up and disappeared from his life two years ago. He seriously couldn't tell if he was dreaming that the woman he'd thought was the love of his life was back or if his loneliness was now making him see mirages of her. As he was staring at her Bunz looked down at his big-ass dogs. Neither of them growled, but they were staring back at her. She remembered them, though, from when they were puppies. She wondered if they remembered her.

"Can you say something, please?" Bunz pleaded, trying to keep tears from falling again.

"Wh-wh… how… where… maaaaaan," Eric stuttered, at a real loss for words. It took him almost a minute to get his

27

thoughts right, then he managed to speak. "You look horrible; what the heck happened to you?"

Bunz sighed. "I… uh… had a really rough couple of days," she told him, deciding not to dive too deep, now was not the time. "I am so sorry to just pop up, but I couldn't…I…I missed you…so much, E."

He looked at her again, feeling perplexed by her. He thought she was gone. He'd been broken for months after she left, and now she was back. He couldn't wrap his brain around it. But the bruises and swollen eye temporarily made his anger dissipate and replaced it with compassion.

"Come in, Mo-Mo," he told her, calling her by the nickname he'd given her, back when things were great between them.

"I…um…I don't want to interrupt you, if…you have a woman in there, Eric," Bunz replied even though the thought nearly killed her.

"The only woman that lives here is that one," he said, pointing to the 2-year-old female bully, "LaLa hasn't ever been a fan of another woman comin' into my house; she must remember you, because if she didn't, you'd already be bleeding."

He took a moment to just look at her. It made her feel shy for some reason but somehow him pulling his attention away from her was worse. "Why are you drivin' this?" he questioned taking in the pickup that was very much not her style.

"Um," Bunz looked at it, "I kind of stole it."

"From where?"

"Reno."

Eric's eyes went wide with shock. "Reno…*Nevada?!*"

She nodded her head.

"You drove a fuckin' *stolen* pickup truck all the way from out there to *here?*" he questioned like she had lost every bit of sense he ever thought she had.

"I *had* to, E! People were after me!" she defended.

"Maaaaan, what the fuck was you doin' out there, girl?" he asked even if he wasn't sure that he wanted to know.

"Can we go inside, please? I'll tell you everything, I swear! If you don't want me here afterwards then I just ask that you let me spend the night so I can get some real sleep before I go!" she damn near begged.

Eric groaned before he released a big sigh feeling nothing but frustration. He handed her his shotgun before going to the truck and grabbed all her bags for her, told her to follow him, then led her and his dogs around the corner to the side door entrance.

They stepped inside a plain kitchen, with painted wood cabinetry, and linoleum tile floors. Eric closed and locked the door behind her, dropped her bags in front of the refrigerator, then stood, folding his arms over his barrel chest.

"I'm all ears," he told her.

Bunz took a deep breath then she began telling the only man she had every truly trusted *everything*.

She met him 2-and-a-half years ago, down at the club in Chicago she'd danced at, and it was love at first sight. They became friends, then lovers. It was great. They knew they were made for each other and were inseparable. Even with all of that she still hadn't been able to come to terms with the belief that she could get her *happily ever after*. To her it just wasn't real. Especially with a drug dealer who had more groupies than he knew what to do with because he was rich.

On top of that he was sexy. Eric had the skin tone of creamy peanut butter and long hair that was somehow three distinct shades of brown that lived in a curly afro style. His strong manly face could easily get him into GQ magazine, or any other popular magazine that showcased the world's most handsome men. His lowly-trimmed beard was sharply lined and looked tattooed on.

And his body was downright sinful. He was built, the countless hours in the gym showed on his body. Add that to the fact that he ate right, avoided fatty meats like pork, and had never and would never try from his own supply and he was damn near perfect physically.

Eric was the same age as her, they even shared a birthday. Add that too everything else that they had in common, and you couldn't tell them that the Man above hadn't built them for each other. Eric wanted everything with her, being the power couple, *everything*. And if you would've asked him he would've said that she did too... but she left, after everything they had been through, good and bad, just when he thought they were really in it... she dipped.

After that Eric swore, he would never give his heart to any bitch ever again. He started living by the motto *Bitches ain't shit but hoes and tricks*, dogging hoes left and right, treating women like pieces of meat, not giving a fuck about tears and begging for affection. He tricked a little bit of dough on them, then got the dome or pussy, and left them high and dry.

But the woman in front of him, the sweet, beautiful woman that he had shed tears and blood for...she was his weakness. He couldn't deny her, even if he wanted to.

***

Eric sighed to himself after she finished telling him what was going on. He just looked at her for a long minute and thought about the hell she had been through. Her beautiful face was bruised, her right eye was swollen and by the way she had been limping, he could tell she was injured beyond what showed on her face.

"Okay... aight," he said, "what's your plan now?"

Bunz shrugged; she didn't have a full plan. "Try to get these diamonds sold off, then...I don't know."

Eric suddenly left out of the kitchen, heading off up a short flight of carpeted stairs to the upper level, where his three bedrooms were. She didn't follow him, instead she just stood there with a gun in her hand and the dogs ignoring her completely. Maybe he was about to tell her to get the fuck out. Just as she was about to grab her bag and figure out something else Eric came back down the stairs, talking on the phone. Bunz listened to what he was saying as he came back into the kitchen.

"Yeah, at my crib, bro. As soon as possible," she heard him say.

Seconds later, he ended the call.

"Wh-who was that?" she asked nervously.

Eric looked at her with furrowed eyebrows. "Don't do that, Mo-Mo," he told her, hearing the trepidation in her voice, "my gauge is loaded and in *your* hands. I know you'd use it if you felt the need to, but you don't. Now to answer your question that was a guy I know that I handled business for a few times that has a chop shop. He's gon' come get that firecracker red ass Ford and take it far away from here. As for you, tomorrow when you wake up I'ma take you to my salon so you can get some relaxation while you get a little pampering. You've been through a *lot*, and I feel you deserve some peace."

Bunz's eyes began welling up with tears again. The gratitude she felt for his generosity was beyond anything she could describe with words. He had accepted her back into his home, even if just for a day or two, and had already started helping her out with her problems.

"Grab those thangz and bring 'em with you; I have a safe you can put them in, so you'll know they're safe until we can find you a buyer," Eric said.

"We?" she asked him, with puzzlement.

"Yeah, Monique. Aye, man. I know who Barry Paulmatti is, Mo-Mo; he was not a plain mobster. Stealin' diamonds like those and killing him...you gon' have the hardest time finding a buyer that won't set you up to be killed by people still out to avenge him or rob and kill you themselves."

Bunz got the diamond necklace and the bagged diamonds out of her bag and followed him up the stairs, to his biggest guest bedroom. Inside, it had the same cream-colored carpet as the whole upper floor did, with white walls, wood furnishings, and a closet with a bending mirror door.

Eric slid the mirror door open, then stepped in. Standing in front of what seemed like a plain wall, he pressed on a spot. A false panel of drywall slid away, revealing a high-tech safe, equipped with an eye-retina scanner, along with a number pad under it.

Bunz watched him enter a code. The safe started beeping, then a digital voice announced, "Please enter new code now".

"Come enter a code, then put your eye to the scanner," Eric instructed.

He stepped out as she stepped in. Bunz did as he told her. When the put her own code in, and put her right eye to the scanner, the door opened. She put the necklace and bag inside before shutting it and committing her code to memory. Once she was done, she turned back to Eric. She stepped into his line of sight making sure to make eye contact.

"Thank you, E," Bunz said, trying to keep her emotions in check.

Eric looked down into her beautiful doe-like eyes. He smiled, then wrapped his arms around her, hugging her to his rock-hard body. It'd been so long since she felt the safety and comfort of him. It made her lose control of her emotions. For the second time in as many days she broke down. Tears flooded her face as she sobbed a mix of letting go and feeling safe taking over.

Eric let her get it all out, holding her until she started regaining control. When she stopped crying, he held her by her shoulders, told her to take a deep breath, then he spoke.

"I'ma go draw you a bath, and while it fills up, I got a cold steak for that eye. Make yourself at home, Mo-Mo."

He left then, to go run her a hot bubble bath. He came back with the cold steak for her eye, and his sawed-off, giving it to her, so that no matter if it was in the tub, on the toilet, or brushing her teeth, protection was within reach.

With clean undergarments, some hygiene products, Bunz was led to the bathroom, where Eric had lit the candles that lined the ledge surrounding the tub. They gave off a peach scent that worked in sync with the small MP3 player that had the soothing sounds of a tropical rainstorm coming from its speakers. Eric made sure the fluffy towel, robe, and the loofa were to her liking. He set the gun on the tub, and then he gave her some privacy, stepping out of the bathroom and closing the door.

Bunz closed her eyes, and for a minute, spoke to the Man above, thanking Him for delivering her back to Eric, asking for Him to forgive her for all that she'd done, and all that she was likely to have to do in the future. With her prayer finished she stripped down and slid her aching body into the steaming hot bubble bath. The water soother her body while the sound of rain did the same to her mind and she drifted off to sleep.

***

When Bunz opened her eyes, she discovered that she was in the guest bedroom, laid out in the bed, wrapped in the fluffy comforter. She didn't even remember getting out of the tub. Feeling something down by her feet, she looked and saw that one of Eric's dogs was stretched out comfortably with her. When she moved, he lifted his head and looked at her. She went to sit up only to feel a pounding in her head. All she could do was groan which caused the 140-pound dog to come to her as if to comfort her.

"Aww, thank you for the kisses; you're sweet," she said, with a giggle as he licked all over her face.

Just then, the female entered the room and jumped her slightly less muscular 108-pound body up onto the bed, joining her bulky mate. She licked Bunz's face with him, helping him make the girl they remembered from their puppyhood happy.

"You two are the shit," Bunz told them, rubbing both of their big meaty heads. She looked at the big, brutish male and said, "I bet E named your big ass something really manly, huh?"

"His name's Deuce."

Bunz looked towards the doorway and saw Eric there, leaning against the entryway in sweaty Under Armor workout apparel. Her jaw nearly dropped at the sight of his bulging muscles. His shoulders were so wide, his chest poked out, and his arms were huge. She could see the lines of his six-pack abs through the tight-fitting workout shirt, as if he wasn't even wearing one. His legs even matched his physique. Bunz remembered how so many men she'd fucked had muscular upper bodies, but their legs looked like twigs.

Eric walked over to the side of her bed. LaLa stood up, tail wagging. He patted her head then looked at Bunz.

"How you feelin'?" he asked her.

"I have a headache, but otherwise, a few hours of sleep did me well."

"A *few* hours?" he asked with a raised eyebrow.

She looked back at him with a raised brow of her own. "Yeah...why you say it like that?"

"Because you been sleep for *more* than 24 hours, Monique."

She gasped. "Oh my God! Are you for real?!"

He nodded. "I'm surprised that you're up now. All that shit you been through, you should be *dead*. But now that you're up I'll make you some breakfast, then we can shoot out to my spot and get you lookin' like the queen I've always known you to be."

"Okay," Bunz said, nodding her head with a faint smile.

He turned to walk off but stopped. "Aye? You still be goin' by that name you had when I met you in the club? What was it... Honey Bunz?"

She chuckled. "Yeah. More so just Bunz."

Eric laughed. "I remember the reason why, too," he shook his head, as the memory of those juicy booty cheeks clapping in his face came back to him, "okay. I'll bring you something for yo' head, then you can meet me down in the kitchen."

Chapter 4

Bunz smashed the heaping plate of scrambled cheese eggs, turkey bacon, cinnamon raisin toast, and followed it up with some passion fruit juice. While she ate, Eric got in the shower then got dressed in a brown Ralph Lauren Polo shirt with a tan horse and rider on his chest, tan cargo Polo shorts, and fresh white low-top Air Force 1s on his feet. His afro was extra curly from the Pink Oil he rubbed into it.

Bunz showered next and dressed in a purple tank-top with Mini Mouse on it, skin-tight high-waist acid washed jeans that emphasized her thick thighs and made her ass look so damn fat. On her feet, she put on white low-top Air Force 1s with purple Nike swooshes. She put her hair into a ponytail, then applied grape-flavored lip gloss to her lips.

Eric knocked on her door before entering. In his hand, he had a flat suede box. Opening it, he showed Bunz a brand-new Taurus 9-millimeter, with three extra 13-round clips inside.

"I want you to keep this with you at all times, Monique. Shits been *real* crazy around *Wauk-Town*, *Zion*, and *Nogo*. These lil' young niggas is out here killin' folks for the dumbest reasons. I need to know that you're safe, even when I'm not around."

Bunz was lost for words. *He still cares!* she thought to herself, on the brink of tears, finding that the very thought of Eric still having feelings for her made her heart start to pound in her chest. She was still gone over him and had dreamed of the day that they would be re-united.

"Th-Thank you, E," she managed to say to him, as she accepted the brand new semi-automatic.

He nodded. "It's all good. You ready to go?"

"Yes," Bunz replied and took the gun out of the case, grabbed a clip and slapped it in, cocking it, then she put the safety on. She tucked it into her purple diamond-stitched leather handbag, along with the other two clips. "I'm ready for whatever," she then added.

Eric smiled. He loved a woman that could handle a gun. There was nothing sexier than a gangster chick.

"Let's ride then," he told her.

Eric got LaLa and Deuce into their leather spiked harnesses and leashes, then he led the three out of the house, to the garage, hitting the remote to open it up.

"Oh wow… that's a nice car," Bunz said, when she saw the gleaming 2022 Bentley Flying Spur, sporting a rare *Silver Lake Blue* paint job and sitting up on custom chrome Bentley rims.

Next to the 4-door was a white 2018 Lorinser edition Mercedes-Benz AMG S65, with charcoal-gray exterior accents, and it sat on 21-inch charcoal-gray Lorinser rims, with a custom body kit.

"Both of them," she added, "you must have really stepped yo' game up since I left, E."

Eric chuckled. "Patience is s virtue. Hard work makes the dream work, and I've ventured into another hustle that brings that *real* gwap in," he told her, holding up the Bentley's keyless start fob and pressing the button.

"And what might that be? Because I could definitely use a job," Bunz told him as the Bentley's twin-turbo V12 purred to life.

"I am what people call… a problem solver."

With a raised eyebrow, puzzled by what he meant, Bunz let Eric take her hand and lead her to the passenger's side of the Bentley. He opened the door and assisted her into the exclusive *Magnolia* leather and Walnut wood trimmed interior. He got his dogs in the back seat, hopped in behind the wheel, then put it in drive. Eric rolled out of the garage, heading for the street. Cruising north, Eric's *little black* phone began ringing. He pulled it from his pocket and answered it.

"Speak on it," he answered.

"Bro, it's Lucci. I need you to go see fat-ass for me, joe. Dude played with my money for *too* long, G. Handle that for me. You know I got you, too."

"Say no more. En route," Eric said to his guy.

He ended the call and tucked the phone back in his pocket.

"I gotta change our plans up slightly, Bunz," Eric told her, as he started plotting on the job that he had just gotten.

"Anything I can do to help?" she enquired, ready to start proving her worth to him.

He looked over at her as he came to a stop at a red light at Lewis and Ridgeland. "It *could* get messy," he informed her, watching her face to see how she would react.

"Messy has been my life for the better half of it," she told him, "ain't no bitch in my blood, E. *Especially* now that I'm here with you. What can I do to help?"

Eric smiled at her, then he told her what he had in mind.

***

"Maaaan, *fuck* that bitch ass nigga Lucci, fam! Fuck he think he is?! A rapper?! That bitch ass nigga can suck a dick for all I care, joe! On the G, fuck him!" snapped Pump. He was a super dark skinned and heavy-set guy with a bald head that resembled a big 8-Ball, and he had a very bad anger problem. "He ain't getting' *shit* from me! His ass goin' to prison for *years!* By the time he gets out, muhfuckas be done forgot about him!"

Rolling up a blunt of some Cookie Kush next to him on the couch in his living room, was Pump's younger nearly identical little brother, Gauge. Across from the two, sitting with their backs to the living room's window, was Dice and Rod. While Gauge was pearling up the Grape White Owl, and his big brother snapped at whoever he was on the phone with, Dice and Rod were weighing and bagging up a kilo of crack-cocaine. They were bagging up everything from $10 dollar rocks to $50 dollar boulders. Their clucks had been blowing their phones up for the past half an hour, dying to blast off.

Pump finally ended the call and tossed it onto the table. He looked at his Rolex, then at Dice.

"Aye, man! Where the fuck yo' guy at with my scratch, joe?! He was supposed to pull up twenty minutes ago!"

'Traffic," Dice said, without looking up from the scale he was using to weigh a chunk of hard with.

"Man, call that slow-ass nigga and tell him go around! It's *my* money and I need it *now!*" Pump continued snapping.

Dice and Rod busted out laughing at him. When Dice hopped up to grab his phone there was a knock at the door causing everyone to pause.

"Which one of y'all dummies got a muhfucka comin' to my spot without tellin' me first?" Pump questioned.

"Not me," Gauge said, putting fire to the blunt to roast it dry.

"Me neither," said Dice.

Rod just shrugged and continued shoving rocks into little sandwich bag corners and tying them up.

"Rod! Go get the door," Pump ordered, reaching down to grab the Draco that was under the couch.

As Rod got up to do as told, Gauge and Dice had grabbed their own mini-Ak-47 pistols, getting ready to dump at whoever as soon as Pump gave the word.

The three watched Rod look through the peephole in the front door.

"Oh shit! Eeeeeee, joe, it's a *baaad*-ass bitch, fam! Damn! She look good than a muhfucka, joe," Rod exclaimed, turning his head and looking at his guys with a cheesy-ass grin, "you want me to-"

BOOM! BOOM! BOOM! BOOM! BOOM!

Five deafening shotgun blasts rang out. The living room's big window shattered to pieces. Dice's head was no longer on his shoulder, but in bloody chunks on the table.

BOC! BOC! BOC! BOC! BOC! BOC!

Semi-auto gunfire blew through the door, hitting Rod so many times that it looked like he was dancing as slug after slug slammed into him. He flew backwards and landed on the floor, blood pouring out of all the bullet holes. Pump and Gauge hopped up and got to shooting. They sprayed out of the window and at the door, sweeping left and right, not giving a damn who they hit. They sent nearly fifty rounds in both directions and still had fifty more.

"HOLD IT!" Pump shouted seconds later, holding his fist up.

Gauge ceased fire.

"Go check it out, lil' bro," Pump told him, listening intently for any sounds of life outside of his house.

Cautiously, Gauge started stepping forward towards the window. As he got to within a few feet of the window, he and Pump heard, *"Psst! Aye, famo!"*

They both turned towards where the living room's kitchen entryway was and saw a tall man, with a curly afro, wearing a skeleton ski mask that hid the lower half of his face. In his hands, he had a sawed-off shotgun, pointed right at Pump.

Before Pump and Gauge could react, a large dog flew through the window and took Gauge down to the floor, mauling the back of his neck. Gauge screamed in pain as the massive XXL Bully's teeth ripped through his flesh like it was boiled meat.

Pump was frozen in fear as he listened to his little brother's blood-curdling screams. Staring at the man with

40

the shotgun, his bladder started to release, soaking the front of his pants.

"Drop it, bitch ass nigga!" the man with the sawed-off demanded.

"A-Aight, joe! Be cool, fam," pleaded Pump, as the dog continued ripping at his little brother.

Pump dropped the Draco onto the couch and raised his hands up.

"Please, man, call yo' dog off my lil' brother," he begged.

"Go open the door," the shotgun holder told him.

Pump hurried to do as told while his little brother begged for the dog to be called off. When he got to the bullet-riddled door, unlocked it, and opened it...

WHAM!

A pistol came flying, bashing him right in the center of his face. His nose broke and blood instantly started gushing.

"Fuuck!" Pump shouted as he flew backwards onto the floor.

Bunz stepped into the house with Deuce and closed the door. As soon as she locked it, she heard the shotgun blast. Looking at Eric, she saw the shotgun's barrel smoking. The guy that LaLa had been mauling no longer had a head.

"Gauge!" cried Pump, seeing the headless corpse of his little brother, bleeding out on the floor.

"Shut the fuck up, bitch ass nigga!" Eric barked, pumping his shotty and pointing it at his face, "you should've thought about this shit before you bit the hand of the man that fed yo' snake-ass!"

Pump's blood ran cold then. He knew the man was talking about how he got out on Domino. He went dead silent, knowing that he was fucked.

"By now, you know what it is, pussy! You owe Domino a 'hunnid gees! Cough it up, and I won't blow yo' head off," Eric told him.

Pump immediately told him where the money was.

"Stay with him," Eric told Bunz, "and if he move an *inch*, if he even *farts*, shoot his bitch ass in the dick!"

Bunz laughed. "Will do," she said, then pointed her 9-millimeter at Pump's crotch.

Eric called LaLa with him and ran into Pump's bedroom, hurrying to find the merch before neighbors started calling the cops, reporting gun shots. In less than a minute, he found the gawp under a false floorboard that had been covered with an area rug. He also found five bricks of raw cocaine, four bricks of heroin, two bricks of fentanyl, and a few diamond chains and watches. He took it all, putting everything on the blanket he snatched off the bed and went back to the living room where Bunz was waiting gun aimed exactly where he'd told her.

"Shoot him," Eric told her.

"No, no, no wai-"

BOC! BOC! BOC! BOC! BOC! BOC! BOC! CLICK! CLICK! CLICK!

She emptied the last of her clip into Pump, sending the last seven rounds into the bottom of his jaw, blowing the top of his head off. Without wasting any more time, Eric gave her the blanket and told her to take it to his car and wait for him.

"I am *not* leavin' you, E," she declared.

He couldn't help but smile at the ride or die chick before him. She had always been down with him, no matter what.

"Aight. Get ready to run, then, gorgeous," he told her.

***

They ran like Mexicans with La Migra chasing them out of the back of the house, into the alley way. LaLa and Deuce were right with them. Just as they got to where Eric parked his Bentley in the driveway of an uninhabited house, halfway down the block from where Pump's trap spot was…

BOOOOM!

The gas vapors leaking from the oven's burners that Eric turned on partially, were superheated by the exploding aerosol can of roach spray that he'd put in the microwave, creating a giant fireball that shot up into the air as the ground shook.

They made it to Eric's car, and hopped in. Eric pulled out of the driveway, driving normally to make sure to not draw any extra attention to the sparkly blue Bentley.

"That was freakin' crazy, E!" Bunz said as he got to 23rd and cut a left turn, "how the hell did you get into that type of work?"

He shrugged. "I'm a dope boy; people know this about me. They also know that I'm 'bout that bullshit these bitch ass niggas be on out in these streets," he told her, coming to a stop at the stop sign at 23rd and Jethro, where Pump's house *was*, up until five minutes ago.

He rolled on, both he and Bunz looking to their left, seeing a crowd of people, all looking at the gaping hole in the ground where the house no longer stood. "Somehow, I became the one people call to rid them of their problems, and they pay a big bag of money to have it not traced back to them."

Bunz was *so* turned on by that G-shit, and even more so because it was *him!* She loved the streets, to be honest, and she loved getting money. The power one had to have in order to be the one that big dogs and other bosses called, seeking *your* help to keep them in business was like being God to her.

Sitting back in her seat, Bunz relaxed, with the thoughts in her head that there was nobody better in life for her than the man next to her, as he made it to Lewis Ave and made a right turn. Now more than ever, all she wanted to do, is prove herself to Eric, and solidify her spot in his life… forever.

Chapter 5

Eric rode out to Kenosha, arriving at a beauty salon that was in a shopping plaza, off Green Bay and Washington. He went around the front of it, riding slow through the packed parking lot. Bunz saw a lot of women inside, most of them getting their hair done, while others were getting their nails done. Next to the salon was a beauty supply store, then a pet store, with a little soul food restaurant at the corner of the business block.

"This is all new, huh? I don't remember any of this being here when…" Bunz stopped talking as she realized she was about to remind him of her dipping out on him.

Eric bent the corner and headed to where the rear of the businesses was. "Yeah, it's all new; I own all of them."

"For real?" Bunz asked in shock.

"Yep. When you make dirty money, it's crucial to clean it up, or otherwise, you lose it."

He pulled up to where a dark blue Dodge Challenger Hellcat Red Eye was parked behind the salon, next to a white Lexus LC 500 Coupe. He told Bunz they were going inside as he killed the engine. He got out and opened the rear door for the dogs to get out. Just as Bunz got out, a white box truck followed by a white H2 Hummer pulled up and stopped right next to them. Eric.

Both vehicles had tinted windows. Bunz couldn't tell who was inside, and pulling up the way they did, she subconsciously went for her gun.

"Relax. They're friends, Mo-Mo," Eric told her, peeping the move.

The box truck's door opened and out came a tall man with long dread locks, and golden-brown skin, wearing a fresh white tank-top that allowed his massive, tattooed chest and python-size arms to be on full display, with Balmain shorts and Timberlands on his feet. Around his neck was a thick long white gold and diamond Cuban link chain, with a charm that said *Steel City Mafia*, and on his wrist, a diamond-encrusted Richard Mille.

He was a *huge* man, muscular like a body builder, with hypnotizing bluish-gray eyes, and a razor-sharp baby hairline and beard.

From the passenger's side, Bunz saw an even taller man that wasn't as bulky as the driver. He was also rocking a fresh tank-top with designer shorts, Tims, and diamond jewelry. He had long dreadlocks, and the same golden-brown skin as the driver. Bunz immediately thought she was looking at the rapper Waka Flocka Flame when she saw him walk around the front of the truck.

"Yeeeooo!" the driver shouted excitedly to Eric, dapping him up with the excitement that could only come from two guys that were good friends.

"My muthafuckin' nigga Macho!" Eric exclaimed, embracing the dread head in a brotherly way, "and Tool! What up, though, big homie!" Eric then said to the taller guy, dapping and embracing him as well.

"What's goodie, bruh?" the giant replied, in a deep raspy voice.

Bunz then heard the doors of the Hummer opening up. She looked back at it and saw an incredibly beautiful woman hop out. She was a *super* thick and statuesque Puerto Rican woman that was just an inch taller than Bunz, without the high-heeled boots she had on. Her caramel-brown skin was deliciously flawless. She wore a bright white halter-style top with blue Gucci symbols monogrammed all over it, a blue cheerleader skirt with white Gucci signs on it, and on her feet, blue lady Timberlands with 6-inch heels. Her long silky hair matched the blue of her designer outfit, and the icy jewelry she sported flickered like a disco ball spinning around. Bunz noticed the big blue diamond ring on the woman's finger and just knew the thing had to cost millions. Knowing a thing or two about colored stones, she had read about purple, red, green, yellow, and blue diamonds.

She was joined by yet another ridiculously thick and stunningly gorgeous woman. She was Puerto Rican as well, with deeper brown skin, like maple syrup. Her silky jet-black hair was braided intricately in a design that Bunz knew had to have taken hours to complete. She was dressed in a form-fitting dress that was blue with *FeFe* in white letters and stars all over it. On her feet were white pointed-toe stilettos, with diamond ankles straps that were as flawless as the ones in her ears, around her neck, and on her wrists.

Last to get out of the Hummer was a woman with a cocoa-complexioned skin tone. Her hair was dreaded like the two men. She was shorter and thinner than the Latinas. She wore a brilliantly white off the shoulder dress, a long diamond necklace with a diamond Hublot on her wrist. She rocked blue pumps on her feet that also had diamond-encrusted ankles straps.

Bunz was truly stunned by the five people. She didn't know who the hell they were, but she did know one thing… they were not plain people.

"Yessy! G-Baby! Tamalita!" Eric shouted out, geeked that the ladies of the Steel City Mafia goons had come to grace him with their presence.

The two Boricuas and the Belizean belle ran to Eric, all three of them hugging and embracing him like it had been years since they had crossed paths. Bunz couldn't help but smile at the sight. It warmed her heart to see that Eric had good people in his life, that really seemed to care about him.

Eric then introduced Bunz to the group. He introduced her to Macho, the blue-gray-eyed wild card of the notorious cocaine importing and trafficking Valdez family. His older brother Tool, the leader of the mob that had been formed in their native home of Pittsburgh, Pennsylvania. Macho's wife, Yessinia, who was from the Bronx, New York, and Macho's girlfriend, Gabriela, who was called G-Baby, and often times, the Gangsta Boo.

Tool's woman Tamalita was born and raised in Belize City, Belize. After introducing her, Bunz noticed that the woman sounded like she had a Jamaican accent.

"It's really nice to meet you, Bunz," Yessy said, as the three ladies all hugged her, "and it's nice to see these two big heads again," she added, speaking of LaLa and Deuce, patting her knee and prompting them to come to her.

While the ladies all showered the dogs with love pats and ear rubs, Eric told Bunz a little about Macho and his brother. When a few things he said made her realize that she had heard of the two Dominican-Puerto Rican goons in the past, along with things dealing with their family, she realized that she was in the presence of billionaire royalty.

"Wow," she said, amazed that she was meeting such famous people. "Um... are we in trouble?" she then asked.

They all busted out laughing.

"Naw, Bunz," Eric told her, "but the competition is as soon as this next shipment hits the streets."

"Fresh in from the tropical homeland, Madam Bunz," Macho told her, "waitin' to turn the summer a few degrees colder. Let's get to it, my nigga," he then said to Eric. "We got more drop offs to make, and so little time."

"Alrighty, then," Eric said, rubbing his hands together, ready to flood the streets with the highly coveted pure Dominican cocaine.

250 kilos of raw were unloaded and stacked into the rear of the salon. Eric went into a safe that was hidden behind a

wall of hair products. He pulled out five big duffel bags, full of cash and handed it to the ladies.

"I'ma get at you, cutty," Macho told Eric, preparing to get back on the road to get to the next drop, "and if you need me for anything, hit my line."

Eric nodded his head. "Ya already know, my boy. Ride safe."

He dapped the two brothers up, then hugged the ladies goodbye. The women all hugged Bunz goodbye after Macho and Tool. They hopped back into their vehicles and pulled off.

***

Eric grabbed the blanket with the merch he had in the whip and entered the salon with Bunz, LaLa and Deuce. He locked the door behind them and applied the high-tech locking mechanism that was bank vault quality. He led Bunz to where another door was hidden by a tall mirror. Sliding it to the side, he entered in a code on the pad lock. The lock popped and he opened the door to a flight of stairs that led down to a subterranean level.

As they descended with the dogs behind them, Bunz could hear 21 Savage's *Bank Account* bumping from inside. At the bottom of the stairs, Bunz gasped in shock when she saw a bunch of women, all of them ass-naked, with Gucci and Louis Vuitton masks on, and gloves.

Some were cooking up coke into crack, some were cutting raw heroin, and the others were either feeding money into money counters, or cleaning and packaging guns.

Eric went to a big circular table and set the blanket on it. He opened it up and instructed a few of the ladies to get the merch and break it all down. Bunz watched a boss work. Her pussy started getting wet from listening to him give the ladies a few other commands, before he dismissed them.

One girl came to get the two kilos of fentanyl.

"You know what to do with them," Bunz heard him tell the girl, then he added, "there's some work upstairs in the salon, too, that needs brought down here asap."

She nodded, then took the fentanyl she and walked off into another room that had plastic pinned up around the entryway, preventing fumes from entering the main area.

Eric then took the cash that he'd retrieved to the money-counter girls, telling them to prioritize it. The diamond jewelry, he took to Bunz and gave to her.

"Put it in your bag. That's all you," he told her.

Bunz gasped. "What? Why?"

"You just helped me out. You deserve it, and from what I know about *Punk*, is that he was ballin', so that shit isn't fake. Plus, you have a meetin' with a friend of mine for those other ones."

Bunz again found herself lost for words. His generosity was amazing to her. She didn't know what to say, nor think.

"Go on 'n put 'em in yo' bag. As soon as I get all this in order down here, we finna head up to the salon so you 'Jolie can get you together."

45 minutes later, the five bricks of coke he brought were turned into ten kilos of crack; the four bricks of heroin were cut with some of the fentanyl and turned into eight, and the rest of the fentanyl was turned into something that would be very useful for Eric in his primary line of work.

The cash had been counted and wrapped in plastic. With everything put back into the duffel bag, Eric took Bunz, LaLa, and Deuce up to the salon through another secret way that ended at a rear office, fitted with two stylist chairs, a makeup station, and a section with for shampooing hair.

Two tall slim and very beautiful women entered the office after Eric closed the hide-away door behind him. They wore flower-print aprons and had fashionable hair styles.

Eric introduced Bunz to them.

"Bunz, this is Anjolie," he said of the light-skinned chick with neatly boxed plait braids hanging loose down her shoulders, "and the dark-skinned stallion is Maxine," he said, of the thick chocolate-complexioned woman with an upswept hair do that looked like it was perfect the BET awards. "Anjie' gon' get you right while Max' braids my hair."

Anjolie greeted Bunz, shaking her hand. "Nice to meet you, Bunz. I have a few books with every hair style ever created. Have a seat and I'ma get you washed, conditioned, and blow-dried, then you can tell me what you want, and I'ma make it happen."

Bunz smiled shyly and got into the comfortable leather shampoo chair. Eric turned on the music and got into his chair so Max could get started on him.

Anjolie leaned Bunz back to the sink and turned on the warm water, as Gold Link's *Crew* featuring Shy Glizzy and Brent Fiyaz started playing. Bunz closed her eyes and felt the water running through her hair. She felt a hand wrap around hers then, fingers intertwining with her own.

Opening her eyes, she saw Eric had taken her hand and was holding it. He looked at her, a warm smile on his handsome face. She smiled back, feeling butterflies in her stomach. She closed her eyes again and relaxed but didn't let his hand go while Anjolie shampooed and conditioned her hair.

***

Half past 6 p.m., Bunz was spun around so she could see what Anjolie had done. She gasped in amazement when she saw her hair and her makeup.

"Holy shit… that's *me*?" she asked, stunned.

Her dark hair had been dyed a rich auburn color, then parted into tiny boxes that plait braids were started from, but instead of single braids, her hair had been twisted into neat locks. Anjolie took the twists, pulled up and wrapped them into a ball on the top of her head, then she snapped with the makeup. She used natural tones to enhance, not change, and the results were truly captivating.

Eric was stuck when he saw her, "Wow… you are… damn, Monique."

Bunz loved it so much that it made her eyes start welling up with tears. "I feel like… like a bum that turned into a boss."

"You were always a boss, Mo-Mo. Especially to *me*," Eric told her.

She looked at him, loving how good he looked with the tiny fishbone cornrows he had in his hair, going straight to the back, the tails hanging down to his shoulders.

"Thank you, E. Thank you so much," she said, trying to keep her voice from breaking.

Eric got up and went to her and gently pulled her from the chair she was in.

"I'm only doin' what a real man does: Lookin' out for you, with no desire for anything in return, other than you getting' to the place in life that you want to be."

Muni Long's *Made for Me* came on as he wrapped his arms around her waist and held her close to him. He smiled as he gazed down into her eyes. Bunz was beyond shy, feeling like a love-struck little girl, in the presence of her first crush or something like that.

Eric tipped her chin up with a finger, making her look up at him making her heart race a hundred miles an hour as he started leaning down. His lips touched hers a second later. Sparks brighter and more colorful than 4th Of July fireworks seemed to go off at that very moment. She swore she could feel little jolts of electricity.

He loved her. He had never stopped, but when she left, he'd buried his heart. No woman had ever gotten close to him like she had. He hoped that this time, he wouldn't wake up to discover that she had left, again. A heart couldn't break twice without the man it was beating inside of breaking with it.

***

Leaving the salon, Bunz was puzzled when she saw that the Bentley was gone, and in its place was a glossy black 2008 Cadillac Escalade Ext pick-up truck, with limo-tinted windows and factory chromed 22-inch Cadillac rims.

"Where's your car?" she asked, as he retrieved the key from a lock box outside of the door.

"Needs a paint job," he told her. "Gotta change the paint when you blow up a house with clowns in it and dip off in a bright blue 4-door Bentley."

She laughed. "Good point."

Eric opened the passenger's door for her and help her up into the ultra-black leather interior, then put the duffel bag in the back row with his dogs. He hopped up behind the wheel and pulled off, getting onto Green Bay Road to head south.

Chapter 6

As daylight began to fade, Eric headed down to South Port Plaza in Kenosha. He parked in the middle of a big parking lot across from a Dollar Tree. Not even a whole minute passed when Bunz saw a dark-green Range Rover Sport pulled up into a spot next to him. The driver, a dark-skinned dread head got out, with a book bag.

The guy hopped into the back with the dogs, unafraid of them. Bunz surmised that they knew him well enough to not even growl. He handed Eric the book bag, and without even opening it up, Eric handed the guy two bricks of dope. They dapped hands then without even a single word being spoken between them, the dread-head got out of the Escalade, got back into his Range Rover and pulled off.

Bunz asked no questions; none were on her mind. All she had inside of her head was to be his ride or die, like she should've been.

***

Back in Illinois, Eric drove to the Hebron apartments in Zion. He dropped off the bricks of crack to his workers there and received bags of cash from what they'd already sold off from his last drop to them.

He then shot over to Beach Park, right next door to Zion, delivering the last six kilos of dope to his heroin guys that pumped a lot of dog food from out of a hotel. Two more bags of cash were put into his whip before he pulled off.

He made one more stop to deliver the plastic-wrapped $100,000 to Lucci's baby momma, then started making his way to the house. As he was en route, he got a call that made him quickly divert his direction. Bunz noticed the quick turn-around and she could see it in his face; Eric was back in beast mode.

20 minutes later, Eric exited off Illinois Route 41 right before he reached Route 173. He turned off and rolled down a dark strip, up to the parking lot of an auto scrapyard. She clocked a few tow trucks and some cars that were marked for sale in the parking lot. Even though she was looking around she failed to notice the dark sedan that was next to two trucks until it flashed its headlights twice.

"This one's gonna' be a little different, Mo-Mo," Eric told her, as he cut his headlights off and came to a stop in front of what Bunz could see was a Crown Victoria.

"Different?" she questioned, when she saw two women, one Black, and one Asian, get out, wearing bullet-proof vests that said, *Illinois State Police*. She tried to mask the fear she felt as she turned back to Eric. "Holy shit, Eric! Are those cops?"

"Yes, but don't freak out; sometimes, they help find people for me. Stay here. This won't take long," he told her.

He reached over and opened the glove compartment. Bunz saw him grab a nasal spray bottle, then get out, greeted by the two gorgeous state trooper chicks.

***

"Whaz' hanin', Yvette?" Eric said to caramel-complexioned Black chick, with her long jet-black hair in a ponytail, then he said what up to her Vietnamese home girl. "JuJu? Y'all lookin' good tonight."

They both chuckled.

"Wouldja' knock it off," said Yvette, "we're in uniform, nigga."

"Exactly my point. All working women are sexy as hell to me," Eric told her.

"Aww, ain't you sweet, E," Julie said with a flirty smile.

"I try. Where's this bitch ass nigga at?" he asked then.

"Trunk," Yvette told him.

Leading Eric to the back of the cruiser, she popped the trunk. Inside was a man, bound by his wrists and ankles, gagged and duct taped. It was the man Eric had been looking for. He'd been one of his workers that he trusted to hold down very large sums of money. A few months prior, the man had for some reason, got sticky fingers, and hit Eric for a significant amount of money, then tried to disappear.

"Our friends down in Chicago caught him tryna hop a plane to Mexico," Julie informed him, "they kept it quiet when we put a few big faces in their pockets."

When the man in the trunk saw Eric, he pissed his pants. He tried begging and pleading, but the sock in his mouth and the duct tape over it prevented it. Eric ripped the tape off his mouth, taking most of his mustache and beard with it.

"E! Come on, man! It wasn't me, bro!" the guy cried, scared shitless.

"Oh naw? You're telling me that it wasn't you that stole $250,000 from my spot, Zip?" Eric questioned, with a raised eyebrow.

"Hell naw! You're my boy, dog! I wouldn't do no snake-ass shit like that! It was Pound, fam! On my momma, joe!"

Eric shook his head. "Wow. *Now* you're snitchin', *and* you're lyin'."

He pulled out his iPhone, went into the archives with video footage of his trap spots. He selected the one where Zip worked and let the man watch himself bite the hand that fed him.

"Lemme' guess... that's not you?" Eric asked, watching the color flush from Zip's face, "didn't know there was a camera there, huh?"

Zip started stuttering with fear, trying to come up with an excuse.

"Save that bullshit, joe. Nobody wants to hear lies," Eric said, taking the nasal spray bottle out of his pocket, "get this bitch ass nigga out the trunk," he then told the lady cops.

"E! Wait! Please!" Zip pleaded as the two badge-wearing gangstresses yanked him out of their trunk and held him steady for Eric.

Eric ignored him and stuffed the nasal spray nozzle up Zip's nostril and squeezed the sprayer. He stepped back; the cops let go of him. Zip fell to his knees, choking and trying to break free of the tape that was holding his arms. The liquefied fentanyl Eric had just shot up his nose was beyond a lethal amount.

The three watched Zip overdose; in twelve seconds, he fell face forward to the ground, dead.

Holy shit! E dun' became a muthafuckin' gorilla since I been gone! Bunz thought to herself, watching him handle business so easily, with real freaking cops supporting him.

She watched the two cops put the dead man back into their trunk, then shake hands with Eric.

"I gotta get like him. If I'm gon' prove to him that I am here to stay, and that I deserve another chance, I gotta be the ride or die chick he needs and wants at his side," Bunz said to herself, just as Eric came to the rear driver's side door of the SUV.

He opened the door and grabbed two big stacks of cash from out of the collection of bags of money that LaLa and Deuce were next to. He handed both cops $15,000 for the assistance. They both gave him sisterly hugs, then hopped back into their unmarked sedan and pulled off to go get rid of the dead body.

"You good?" Eric asked as he started the engine.

Bunz nodded her head.

"Tryna go get somethin' to eat? We ain't ate nothin' all day," he reminded her, just as his phone rang again.

"Hell yeah. I'm starving," she said, then to herself, she thought, *For you.*

Eric answered the call. "What's good, cuzzo?"

Bunz waited as he listened to the caller talk. Less than a minute later, he spoke again.

"What?" he said, with a surprised expression.

He got quiet again as he listened. Bunz wondered who was calling him. Eric shook his head and muttered a curse under his breath. "Yeah. I can help with that. You *sure* you want that to happen, though?"

Uh oh... somebody must've fucked up and pissed the wrong person off, Bunz thought to herself.

"Aight, then, cuz. Check it, I'ma come get you, and *you* can lead on this. I'ma get him up outta there. Be ready by midnight."

Eric ended the call and looked over at Bunz. "I'm drop all this off at the crib then we can go wherever you want. The sky is the limit," he told her, pulling out of the dark lot.

"Um… that's another job you just got?" she asked him.

"Sort of. I gotta teach a lesson to a young knucklehead. Would you like to join me in makin' that happen?"

"Hell yeah!" she exclaimed excitedly, yearning for every opportunity to show him that she was still a ride or die chick… *his* ride or die chick.

"Cool. I'm pickin' my lil' cousin up so she can be the one to handle this issue. We just gon' be there for support," he explained as he got on the road, "you know. It's kind of nice havin' someone with me on these moves. Someone I can trust and that I care about."

Bunz smiled as her heart swelled inside of her chest. She couldn't remember the last time she'd been so happy and felt so… whole. Hearing that he still cared about her out of his own mouth, had her even more ready to prove herself to him.

Whatever he had to do, she wanted in on it so that the memory of any other woman that he had in her absence would be erased and only *she* would fill his mind.

She felt a wet nose nudge her elbow as thoughts of the beautiful life she and Eric could have made her smile so brightly. She turned around and found Deuce's head right there at her arm, sniffing at her.

Turning around, she patted the center console, and he popped his front paws up onto it and got a kiss on the nose from her. He licked her face, making her giggle, then got back down to lay back with his mate.

Bunz turned back in her seat and leaned back, riding comfortably next to the man she never wanted to part ways from again. She reached over and took his right hand into her left, and brought it to her lips, planting a kiss on it.

Eric smiled, then pulled her hand to his, kissing hers. They rode in silence then, listening to the music as it played. The pain of her leaving him was starting to fade away and replacing it was the love he once had for the beautiful queen that he saw in his dreams every time he closed his eyes.

***

After dropping off the money, the jewelry, and the dogs, Eric and Bunz got freshened up for a night out, then hopped into the Benz, shooting down to Chicago for a night on the town. First, he took her to the Cheesecake Factory on Michigan Avenue, where they enjoyed delicious cuisine and glasses of wine. After they dined, they took a stroll down the Magnificent Mile, to the Chicago River. They enjoyed conversation with each other, talking about the future, as the cool breeze from the lake blew through the city. Eric looked at his watch and saw it was time to execute the last job of the night. He filled Bunz in on what it was. She was surprised, but geeked at the same time.

"Let's do it," she said, with a grin.

Eric chuckled at her, "I think you're enjoyin' this more than I am, Mo-Mo."

"Bein' back with you is what I enjoy, E. Everything else is just a bonus," she told him.

Chapter 7

"Maaaan, hell, naw, nigga! Yo' ass tweakin', fam! That bitch lyin'!" said Nikko, as he strolled down north on Joppa with his 4 Corner Hustler homies, en route to get some blunts, and some liquor.

"Nikko, quit cappin', joe. Shortie showed us the video. Yo' ass was cryin' after you smoked that K2 bullshit! All scared 'n beggin' for someone to save you! *And* she put cho' ass on YouTube!" his homie Lil' Solid said, making himself and everyone else laugh.

Lil' Solid, the leader of their little wolf pack, Beezy, Blick, and Dog laughed their asses off at Nikko's salty face.

"Fuck outta here, joe! That *ain't* me! Ain't no bitch got me on camera doin' shit! Fuck you talkin' 'bout!"

"Boy you lie so much yo' teeth gone get to fallin' out," Blick teased as they crossed 24th Street.

15-year-old Nikko was pissed that a bitch had caught him up on camera, crying after smoking a stick of synthetic marijuana that had him petrified from the weird high that it gave him. Being teased by his own guys didn't make it any better. He felt like a straight lame.

"Man, whatever, joe. Aye, what's up with that one lick, though? Them bitch ass niggas on the Hebrons 'n shit," he then said.

The others looked at him, pausing where they all stood.

"Nigga, ain't that yo' uncle's spot?" Beezy asked him.

"Fuck that mean? We mask up and won't nobody know it was me," Nikko replied.

"Fam, yo' ass tweakin' hard. Yo' momma already on yo' ass about bein' out here. She sees you wit' us and she get to tryna blam on yo' lil' young ass," Lil' Solid said, as they started strolling again.

Nikko again felt belittled. His mother stayed on his bumper about hanging with older dudes in the streets. His homies were 21 years of age. They had recruited him into the mob, and after Nikko got his initiation mission completed, successfully, he got his brand and was an official member of the *4 Corner Hustler Vicelord Nation.*

"Fo', miss me wit' all that extra shit. There be a lot of coke and dope up in that spot. All we gotta do is kick the muthafuckin' door in, stick switches in 'erybody face, and take the merch. Who the fuck gon' get crazy when fo' niggas put switches in they faces?" Nikko asked.

Lil' Solid laughed. "Nobody. Aight. Let's make it happen… *tonight!"* he then said.

Nikko's eyes went wide then. He hadn't anticipated Lil' Solid wanting to make the move right away. He at least thought he'd have some time to gather his wits up so he could be ready. He knew how his uncle got down, and everyone under him was just as ruthless.

Fuck this scary-ass shit! We finna go on 'n hit this quick lick real quick and come up fast! On the 4! A nigga can't be broke out here! These hoes don't want no broke-ass niggas, he thought to himself, pumping his head up.

Nikko's thoughts were interrupted when the sounds an engine revving loudly caught his and his guys' attention. On instinct, they all turned around, just in time to see a Cadillac truck screeching to a halt in the street next to him.

Immediately, the front and rear passenger's doors flew open and two figures in all black with masks on hopped out with pistols in their hands.

"Oh shit!!" Nikko and his guys panicked.

Lil' Solid, Beezy, Blick, and Dog took off running in different directions. Nikko attempted to run, but in his haste to get away, he twisted his ankle.

Nikko fell to the ground, grasping his leg, crying like a baby. The two figures walked right up to him and stopped, looking down at him. They both stood over him, clutching their pistols in their hands, eerily silently.

"You's a dummy," the shortest one said.

Hearing the voice, Nikko could tell it was a woman, despite the baggy hoodie and sweatpants she had on. No man had a voice that was as smooth and sweet like that, even making a demand in such a dark demeanor.

"F-Fuck you!" he snapped back.

WHAM!

The shorter of the two kicked him in his side hard, making him yelp in pain.

"Watch yo' mouth, you lil' nigga, before I beat the *shit* out cho' slow ass!" she threatened.

"Get cho' ass up," Nikko heard the second figure demand. It was a woman as well.

"Maaaan, what the fuck?! Who are y'all?! I ain't did shit to no bitches that should have y'all tryna get on that wit' me," Nikko said.

WHAM!

"*Aaagh! Stop kickin' mee!*" Nikko screamed, his ribs hurting like hell now.

The two women went to grab him. Nikko tried to fight them off. The shorter one put his ass in a choke hold.

"Yo! Hold up! Chill," he pleaded, short on breath as the lady's tight grip cut his airway off.

The second chick kicked him in his ankle.

"*Aaagh! What the fuck, bitch?*"

WHAM!

Nikko caught a hard fist to his jaw while the other woman was still trying to choke him out.

"Nigga, what the fuck she just say? Watch yo muthafuckin' mouth!" she yelled.

They both grabbed him and yanked him up off the ground. On his feet, they both stared at him. Nikko tried to hide his fear, but they could see it. The shorter of the two pointed at the open rear door of the Escalade. "Get in the truck. *Now,*" she told him.

Nikko looked at the idling 'Lac truck.

"Hell naw! Fuck I look like?"

SMACK!

"You keep cussin', we gon' keep smackin' and crackin' yo' dumbass, shortie," the tall one said.

Nikko attempted to run again and immediately regretted it when pain exploded in his ankle. The two stepped off after him, catching him in one second. The shorter one clipped his legs from under him and made him fall on his face. Nikko started crying like a little kid then.

"Yeah, cry, *punk!* You ain't so tough now, huh?! All that shit yo' lil' dumbass be on out here in these streets?! I see you wit' them lil' lame-ass wannabe gangbangers! Up to no good 'n shit! Terrorizin' my neighborhood! You think you a goon?! I'ma show you what a real goon looks like, you lil' stupid muthafucka!" the short chick declared.

The two women then muscled Nikko into the Escalade. As they got him back towards the vehicle, Nikko saw that a third figure, this one a man from how big and bulky he was, had gotten out from behind the wheel. He too had a skull-face ski-mask on. In his hands, he had a bag.

The sounds of growling averted his eyes to the open rear door. Nikko glanced that way and saw the two big devilish-looking dogs in the rear of the Cadillac truck. He nearly pissed his pants when he saw they were staring right at him.

"What the hell do y'all want with me? Why is y'all takin' me?" he pleaded to know.

The three gave him nothing. The male figure put the bag over Nikko's head while the two ladies held him in place.

Everything went dark and the next thing he knew, a hand clamped over his nose. He started smelling the strong odor of chemicals. In mere seconds, Nikko felt himself losing consciousness. Seconds later, he was out like an amateur boxer going against Floyd Mayweather.

Nikko was tossed into the rear of the SUV with the dogs. The ladies jumped in with him. The man hopped back behind the wheel and peeled off, speeding off to take Nikko somewhere a little more discreet.

***

Sometime later, Nikko started to regain consciousness. He instantly remembered that he had been snatched up by three masked up people, who hadn't told him what they wanted. The fact that they were wearing masks told him that they wanted something and needed to hide their identities to get it, or else, he would already be dead. He learned that from his mother, who had been taught the ways of the street from a cat she grew up with, who was like a brother to her, and an uncle to him.

Nikko's body tilted as the car took a left turn onto what he was sure was a gravel road. Gravel meant that he was no longer in the hood and that made him more than a little nervous. After a few minutes he finally heard the engine cut and doors starting to open. Everyone was getting out including the dogs. *Damn what the fuck was going on?*

"Let's go, lil' nigga! Time to pay for your sins," he heard one of the women say.

He was yanked out of the SUV then and thrown on the ground.

"Maan, what the hell do you want! I ain't on shit out here! I'm just a kid!" he angrily snapped, wishing he could see where he was.

He heard chuckles then.

"You hangin' around with the *wrong* people, dummy! Yo' bitch ass homeboys ran and left you hangin'. Real niggas would've got to poppin' at us to save yo' send-off ass, but naw. Them niggas ran like cowards," he heard the short chick say.

The more the woman talked, the more she sounded familiar to Nikko.

"Get up," he heard her snap then.

"How the fuck I'ma do that?! I'm tied up and my leg is killin' me!"

"Nobody gives a fuck!" the woman snapped.

Nikko felt the press of the barrel at his temple.

"Get the fuck up nigga! *Now!*"

Nikko mustered the strength that he had and did his best to rise from off the ground. It took almost a minute, but he managed to get up to his feet. The bag was then removed from his head. He saw the three figures in front of him, standing with their pistols in their hands, a few feet away from him. After a quick glance around, he could see that they had brought him to a park that was ducked off far from any road he could see,

"Didn't yo' momma teach you better than the shit yo' lil' young ass is out here doin'?" the male figure asked, finally speaking for the first time.

Nikko swore that he sounded familiar too. He just couldn't place their voices no matter how hard he tried.

He sucked his teeth and waved the guy off. "My momma ain't here, fam! I'm gettin' it how I live! Who the fuck is *you* to question *me*?" Nikko asked, attempting to put up a brave front, though he was terrified and trembling in fear.

"Who am I?" the man asked, with a chuckle.

He stepped up, closing the gap of space between himself and Nikko. He towered over the young boy. His presence intimidated Nikko. He could *feel* the anger inside of the masked man radiating off of him like a campfire that he had gotten to close to.

"*I* am the nigga that will slap the *dog* shit out cho' ass if you say one more dumbass thing, or, if you keep talkin' like you'sa gangsta."

"Man, I *am* a muhfuckin' *Solid 4 Corner Hustler*, fam! And if I'ma die tonight, then I'm finna *die* like a muhfuckin' Solid Fo'! Ain't *no* bitch in my blood, joe!"

The short chick laughed. "Y'all hear this nigga?" she said to the other two. "He got *three* guns on his ass, and he *still* tryna play tough. Man, *fuck* this lil' dumbass nigga! Let's just get it over with and leave his stupid ass here for coyotes to eat!"

Nikko then saw the man and the other woman shake their heads.

"So young and handsome," Nikko heard the tall woman say.

"And yet so muthafuckin' *dumb!*" the short chick said, shaking her head as well.

The three of them raised their guns, pointing at Nikko's face. Nikko's heart dropped as he realized his life was about to end.

The short chick began counting down, "Five… four… three…"

Nikko closed his eyes as the woman counted. Suddenly then, all the horrible things he had done in his life flowed into his mind. Gangbanging, jumping on people, shooting shit up; everyone he had robbed, did dirty, whether it was family or friends; all the times he had gotten locked up and had to have his mother come get him out. All the times he had made his mother cry. He had never known his father. The only significant male figure he had ever had in his life was his uncle.

Nikko's entire life of crime flashed before his eyes. It wasn't long at all. Above all else, he remembered how he had *wanted* to be a successful businessman, just like his uncle. He had wanted to have a bad-ass chick in his life, like his uncle had the last time he'd seen him. He wanted to get married, have kids, a dog, a nice house, and a few fly rides.

Regret filled him. He thought about his mother and how she was going to go crazy when his body was discovered, wherever these people decided to leave him.

It was over now. He had royally screwed up.

"Two… one… blast off!" the short chick shouted.

Nikko took a deep breath and waited for the first bullet to hit. He whimpered as he wondered how bad it was going to hurt and how long the pain would last before he died. What would it look like when he was dead. Was God going to let him through the gates or was the *red man* going to be poking at him with his pitch fork, making him a slave for all eternity?

A second later, instead of feeling the white-hot pings of pain he'd always heard people say it felt like Nikko felt cold liquid splashing his face. He opened his eyes and saw that the three people… were shooting *water* guns, painted black, at him.

"What the fuck?" he questioned, wondering if he was tripping, or did he get shot and die and think he was getting squirted with water guns.

Right then, the three masked figures then pulled their masks up, revealing their faces. Nikko's jaw dropped when he saw his big cousin there, with a female that had long rust-colored single braids, and his mother.

"E…Eric? *Mom?*" he gasped, stupefied with shock.

Eric, Bunz, and Tracy laughed their asses off at the stupefied look on Nikko's face.

"What up, lil cuz?" said Eric with a smile, "that's really crazy that you couldn't tell it was us by the sounds of our voices."

Nikko was so flabbergasted that he couldn't even speak.

"Check it, lil' nigga," continued Eric, stepping up to him. "Why is my lil' sister tellin' me that you been out here actin' *real* crazy lately, joe? Fuck's up with that?"

Nikko swallowed hard. "C-Cuz… I'm just… I was just tryna get money," he explained, looking at the third chick, trying so hard to figure out where he knew the woman from.

"That's yo' excuse?" his mother Tracy asked, shaking her head, "I should smack the fuck out cho' ass, Nikko. You sound dumb. How is it you don't realize that we ain't broke?! Nigga I got plenty money! Fuck you need to be in the streets for?!"

"Because ma! Uncle Eric always told me to not ever let a woman take care of me! That I am the one that's supposed to take care of my woman!"

"I am your mother, *not* your woman. I am supposed to take care of you Nikko!" Tracy yelled.

Eric and Bunz stayed silent. It was stupid but at the end of the day he just wanted to be seen as a man. Especially in the eyes of his mother and they could respect that. There were better ways to do it, ways that didn't involve him putting himself at risk but that was real. Tracy took a moment and came to the same conclusion. She fought back tears at the thought that her baby boy just wanted to take care of her.

Shaking his head, as Nikko found the ability to move, he couldn't help but to chuckle at his own damn self. He'd never been so scared in his whole life. He said a silent thank you to the man upstairs that he didn't have to use the bathroom because he would've shitted himself. And he knew they would've never let him live that down.

"Y'all really just got me, though… that is crazy," Nikko said, in utter disbelief.

"Yahp!" Tracy said, wiping her eyes, chuckling as she had the image of his terror-stricken face burned into her mind forever. "You deserved it. You lucky we all still love you to death. There are people related by blood that would've murked yo' ass *for real*, baby."

Nikko shook his head. His shoulders slumped down. He felt so ashamed.

"So, what chu' gon' do now, Nikko?" asked Eric, "you still want that street life? 'Cause next time niggas snatch you up, you know, like opposing gang members... the jump out boys... they probably ain't gon' be doin' no intervention-type shit like this."

Nikko shook his head. "I can't do this anymore. This street shit...," he paused, seeing the look on his mother's face when he cursed, "I mean, this street stuff is *too* much, joe." Tears filled his eyes then and ran down his face, "I could've really just died right now."

Eric nodded his head, "Smart man. Time waits for nobody. Get in the car and we'll drive you and yo' moms back to the crib."

Chapter 8

Eric made his way back up to Lake County, hopping off the highway and shooting west to Zion. With Bunz riding shotgun and his younger cousins and dogs in the back he headed towards where Nikko and his mother lived.

During the ride, Nikko was introduced to Bunz. When he heard the name, he lit up when all recollection of when Bunz was around, before she had disappeared, came flowing right back to him.

"Bunz! You're back," Nikko exclaimed, reaching up and wrapping his arms around the woman.

She smiled and giggled, loving the enthusiasm, "nice to see you again, Nikko. Hope the next time we link up it's not gon' be to teach you another lesson."

"Or comin' to visit you in an ER because you got yo' young ass shot," Tracy added.

"Tracy, that's enough now, cuz. He gets it," Eric said, coming to Nikko's defense.

"Don't do that, E. He *really* deserves to get his ass slapped six times," Tracy told him.

Eric and Tracy had grown up together. Tracy had been taught by him to be tough and fearless. She could be just as ruthless when it came to handling business. She didn't play no games and didn't expect none to be played on her.

"I think now, Nikko's gon' fly straight and let the street shit be for the street niggas and bitches. Right, lil' cuz?" Eric asked him, as he turned onto Tracy and Nikko's street.

"Yes. I'ma go get a job."

Bunz smiled at that.

"Mhmm. We hear you talkin' lil' boy. Be 'about it, don't talk about it," Tracy told him, then left it alone.

Arriving at a house by the corner of Salem and Lewis Ave, Eric pulled into the driveway and parked up by the built-in single-car garage.

"I got a package ready for pick up whenever you want it, big cuz," Tracy said to him, as she and Nikko got ready to hop out.

"I'll swing by and grab it tomorrow," Eric told her.

Tracy nodded, then looked at Bunz. "Glad to have you back, girl. Yo' ass better not leave again, or this time, I'ma hunt yo' muhfuckin' ass down myself and put my foot up that fat ass booty you got."

Bunz chuckled and raised her hand up, "I swear it on my life, I'm here to stay, Tracy."

Tracy nodded, reached in, and hugged her then she and her son walked off. Eric waited for the two to enter their home and then backed out of the driveway. He rolled off, feeling good about hopefully saving the young boy's life with a valuable lesson.

Tired from a long day of solving problems, getting money, he was ready for bed, and he figured Bunz was ready to turn in as well. But she had other things on her mind

***

After entering the house with the dogs, Eric and Bunz and got by LaLa and Deuce settled in. They showered them both with love and affection. They rubbed the dogs down, making their legs and tails go wild with excitement. Eric gave them big turkey bones to gnaw on, then rising back up, he saw Bunz, leaning against his fridge, gazing at him.

He was truly in awe of her. Her new hair style made her look so much like a queen. Even in the baggy sweats, she looked mouth-watering. He couldn't help but bite his bottom lip as he took in her beauty. He wanted her… *badly*.

Bunz gazed at him with lust, desiring him in the worst way. He was so thuggishly handsome to her, His thuggish swagger had her yearning for him.

Eric went to her, pulling her body to him before he leaned down and pressed his lips to hers. She kissed him back as her soul ignited with such a fierce fire that only he could put out. He deepened the kiss, as he pushed her against the fridge. She lifted her left leg and wrapped it around him, grinding her pussy on his leg. Her nipples were hard and aching while her clit throbbed, dying for some simulation. She was hot and ready for him to fix all of that for her all night long.

After a long moment she pulled back and looked up into his eyes. They were full of liquid desire and his pupils were blown and it was all for her.

"I want you so bad, E," she told him, her emotions threatening to break loose as her heartbeat in her chest for the man in front of her.

"You have me, Monique," Eric told her, in a low deep tone of voice that made her temperature rise sky high. "The question is, do I really have *you*?"

She nodded her head, "Yes. I swear you do, baby. You have all of me."

Eric smiled and reached up to softly stroke her face.

"Then let me take you up to my bedroom, and we can have each other, over, and over, and over again."

Bunz kissed his lips again. "Take me, Eric! Right *now*," she begged him.

Eric scooped her up into his arms and ran her up the stairs, to his bedroom, to do what they both had been wanting since she popped back up out of nowhere.

***

"Damn! Ooooo, shit! E! Yeeesss!" she cried out, as Eric sucked on her clit like eating pussy was his real profession, instead of killing people and selling drugs, "Fuuuuck, baby! Oh, my God it feels so good!"

"It tastes so good, baby," Eric hummed against her, his breath tickling her swollen and super sensitive pussy lips.

He went back in, aiming to make her remember all the times before. Somehow, he felt like he had failed her, which may have been the reason she left. A woman that is truly happy with her man will *never* leave him, no matter what.

The Dream's *Luv Songs* crooned from the surround sound speakers in his lavish bedroom. The mood was set, and the vibe was perfect. Now he was on a mission to solve the problem he'd had all day.

He dined on her, pleasing her to no end. He made her head spin as he ate her up. Inserting two fingers inside of her, he stroked her tight walls, stimulating her, making her *crave* penetration. In minutes, Bunz reached her climax and cried out as she exploded all over his hand.

Eric was ready to feel her, all of her that he had missed. He rose up from between her legs, his face dripping with her release. All she could do is stare at the sculpted masterpiece in front of her. He was perfect in every way that mattered to her.

Before he could slide inside of her, she slid her body down the bed. It was his turn to be the focus, she wanted to make sure she pleased him now because he had damn sure pleased her. She wrapped her hand around his 9" tool before bringing her lips to the bulbous tip. She kissed it first just to show her appreciation before swirling her tongue around the tip. Bunz took her time as she dragged her tongue from base to tip on the underside of his shaft and back down to his balls.

"Ooooohhhh *shhhhhhheeeeeiiiit!*" Eric's eyes crossed when he felt her take his balls into her mouth and suck on them, "*goddamn*, I missed you, Mo-Mo! Fuuuck!"

Bunz sucked on his nuts for a minute, then spit them out. She scooted back onto the bed, ready for him. She opened her legs up wide, letting him see that goodness gracious between her thick thighs. Beckoning to him, she curled up a finger and invited him to her.

Like he was hypnotized by her, Eric got onto the bed and crawled on top of her. She reached down to grasp his hardness, putting it to her soaking wet box. He felt that warm wet tunnel that he remembered always made his eyes roll to the back of his head.

As he entered her, Usher's *Superstar* started playing. Bunz gasped when he eased his way into her, stretching her walls until she fit him like a glove. A firm reminder that they were a perfect match.

"I'm glad you came back to me, baby," Eric told her, as he paused, staring down into her eyes with his dick all the way inside.

She smiled up at him. "I'm never leaving you again, Eric. I… I love you," she told him, admitting what she had been thinking since she was scheming on the diamond man, "I love you so much that I can't even forgive myself for leaving you like that until I know that *you* forgive me."

Eric gazed down into her eyes for a minute, then he smiled again. "I forgive you, Monique. I do. And I love you, too," he told her, meaning it from the bottom of his heart, "I can't lose you again. That shit almost killed me when you left."

Tears began wetting her eyes. She'd been so guilt ridden for so long. When she came back, it got worse, seeing that he so easily allowed her back into his life, despite how she got down on him. More than anything, she wanted to prove to Eric that she was down with him, for life.

"To a new us?" she asked him, hopingly.

Eric nodded his head. "Yes. Now, lemme' show you how happy I am that you're back in my life," he told her. "Again," he added.

Then he did repeatedly until the sun rose up. Out of gas, they passed out in each other's arms, naked, fulfilled, and madly in love.

***

Eric woke up around 8 o'clock that evening and discovered that Bunz wasn't next to him. He shot up feeling panicked, dreading to think that she had bounced on him. When he smelled the mouth-watering aromas of something frying in the air and the sounds of his dogs running around, he sighed with relief, realizing that she was still there.

He laid back down and, for a minute, closed his eyes and thanked the Man above for bringing his angel back to him. After his prayer, he got up, threw on his boxer briefs and his shorts, and headed out of the bedroom to go see what she was cooking up.

Making his way down to the kitchen he could see LaLa and Deuce playing tug-of-war with a big turkey bone. They were growling, going at it for real, competing for the bone. He shook his head, chuckling at the two beasts, acting just like a man and a woman that loved each other.

When he reached the landing of the main floor, he bent the corner and entered the kitchen. He skidded to a stop when he saw Bunz, frying chicken and crinkle cut French fries. She wore one of his shirts and nothing else.

LaLa and Deuce dropped their bone and ran to him, tails wagging, grunting and barking for him to play with them. Eric patted their heads, but his attention was on the sexy belle in his kitchen, frying chicken, wondering what she had on under his shirt.

Bunz turned to him. With a seductive smile, she spoke, "Hope you're hungry, baby; I'm makin' your favorite."

Eric walked up to her and wrapped his arms around her from behind. He planted a soft kiss on her neck, then spoke close to her left ear.

"You are my favorite, Mo-Mo," he said, then his hands slid down to her hips. "Can I have another taste? That pussy was so good that you got me feenin' for more."

She bit her bottom lip. Just that quick she was wet and ready for him. She moved quickly, turning off the burners and pushing the pans off the heat. She turned so that her body was closer to his and she could look up into the eyes she loved.

"Eat," she told him.

In four seconds, she found herself on the counter and his shirt off, thrown somewhere. He pushed her legs out as far as they could go before he dove in headfirst. He was swimming in the pussy like he was Michael Phelps or something.

Eric devoured her until she exploded on his face, drenching it. By then his dick was hard and throbbing, damn near begging for a release. He yanked her body off the counter and made her grab the edges of the smooth countertops. She moved however he wanted easily, causing him great joy. He kissed her neck, down her shoulder, upper back and continued making his way south until the ass he loved so much was in his face.

Bunz squealed in delight when she felt him open her ass and run his tongue up her crack.

"Ooooo, E! Shit! Oh, fuck!" she cursed, goose bumps forming all over her from the hot and naughty toe-curling sensation.

Eric swirled his tongue around her asshole, making her head spin. She rose up onto her tippy toes as he juices ran down her leg. Never had another man turned her on like Eric did, *never.*

***

"Wow... look at him go... he's really tunin' her up, eh?" said Jimmy J, as he and his partner Sosa sat in Jimmy J's car, in the driveway of a house that nobody lived in, across the street from where their boss had tracked the target to.

Watching them through binoculars, they saw the braided-up man on his knees in the kitchen, eating their target's ass. Jimmy J's dick got hard as he watched. So, did Sosa's.

"Yeah, he's gonna make her head explode doin' that type of stuff. I wish my bitch lemme' do that to her," Sosa said, "she's such a fuckin' nun."

Jimmy J laughed, "Should we let 'em finish? It *is* their last night on earth."

"Fuck that. Let's just kick their shit in, make 'em cough the rocks up and blow their brains out so we can get back. I hate Illinois."

"So be it," Jimmy J said.

The two contract-killers reached into the back seat of the Impala and grabbed their fully automatic AR-15s, both equipped with miniature double-side drums, loaded with one hundred rounds of 5.56s.

"Alrighty, then, Sosa," Jimmy said, as they got out, locked, loaded, and protected with Kevlar, "let's got earn our next kill and collect our money."

The two crept towards the house, using the darkness of the early night sky to advance right up on their targets. They had a mission to complete, and there was no room for failure.

Chapter 9

Eric power-fucked Bunz from the back with her twisted-hair wrapped around his left hand, while he smacked on her ass with his right. She moaned, cried out, cursed repeatedly as he put it on her like a straight G. He pounded her hard and fast. It sounded like someone was in the kitchen, clapping their hands at their performance.

Bunz was seeing stars, while she smelled the delicious chicken and French fries that were just inches away from her.

"Ooooohhhh, yeeesss baby! Yeeesss, hit this pussy, Shiiitt!" she screamed out.

Eric gritted his teeth as beads of sweat dropped from his forehead, splattering on her ass. He could feel the muscles in his back tightening up. His nuts started tingling, dick pulsating inside of her.

"Woooo fuck!" he yelled as he felt his nut coming.

Bunz exploded first, cumming all over his dick. That pushed him closer to the edge, he was ready to cum when Deuce and Lala started going crazy. Their actions made him stop immediately. The dogs jumped up and ran into the living room barking aggressively. Eric and Bunz looked at each other confused until they heard the deafening sounds of an assault rifle going off.

"Knock, knock!" Jimmy J yelled after he and Sosa blew *the living room window out with their guns, "housekeeping, at your service!"*

Sosa laughed his ass off at his partner as they stepped into the house, "*yeah, we are here to clean up the mess for you!*"

The two Italians used the cover that the darkness of the night brought. They wanted minimal neighbor interference, so they stayed low, moving with precision. They'd heard two dogs, so they were also on the lookout for them, the target, and had to make sure to keep their ears open.

Creeping through the living room, Jimmy J went straight, while Sosa cut to the right, to enter the kitchen. They met back at where the landing to the stairs to go upstairs to the bedrooms and downstairs to the subterranean game room was. Jimmy J told Sosa to check downstairs and he was going up. They split off, gun barrels up, ready to spit at anything moving.

"*Hellooo, Madam Diamond Thief! Where art thou?*" Jimmy J called out, "*don't be scared, I'm only here for the diamonds!*"

Even as he said it, he gripped the AR-15 tighter as he stepped into a small bedroom to his left and looked around. He saw nothing, so he went into the bedroom that was ahead to his left. He saw women's clothing there and knew it was where the girl was sleeping. He looked at a pair of panties on the bed, went to them, and smelled them.

"Mmmm! Sweet," he said to himself, then he saw the mirror closet door.

With a grin on his face, he went to it and opened it. Clothes on hangers filled the closet. He cursed under his breath and left out, cutting to the left and entering the last bedroom. He immediately saw an old safe on top of a tall dresser, with a combination lock.

"Bingo! Let's get this thing cracked open and see what we got," he told himself, setting his gun down on the bed, and getting a small tool kit from his belt.

***

Sosa searched around the lower level of the house. He looked behind the bar first, then the half bathroom, then the utility room that was next to it. Coming up empty, he went and stood in the middle of the game room. He looked around and saw the door to the laundry room in the far corner. He smirked to himself and started towards it.

"Heeeey, diamond girl!" he said to the door, pointing his AR at it, "I know one thing; if I find you behind this door, and you refuse to give up the diamonds, you're gonna have a *big* problem!"

Sosa then reached out to grab the knob and open the door. As soon as his skin touched the knob he yelped out in pain as 70,000 volts of electricity gave him the shock of his life. He was launched backwards, smacking into the wall. Before he hit the ground, completely immobilized.

Shaking and trembling, Sosa then heard the door open. Seconds later he saw a pair of Nikes and he managed to look up and see the light skinned man with braids that had his face buried in the girl's ass crack, shirtless, with a pair of Nike basketball shorts on, holding two Glocks in his hand, and behind him was the woman he and his partner were after, with a blanket wrapped around her, and two big ass pit bulls.

Eric raised his guns, pointed at the man and squeezed the triggers, blasting him repeatedly, rocking him to sleep forever.

"Problem solved, cracker," he said through clenched teeth.

"What about the other one, E?" Bunz asked, trying to hold the blanket closed around her naked body.

"I got him. Stay here with the dogs," Eric told her then crept off to catch the other guy that he was sure was on the way to check on his partner.

As he tried to get the safe open, Jimmy J heard Sosa's screams, then seconds later, he heard the gunshots. He immediately grabbed his gun and took off out of the bedroom to get to the stairs.

"*Sosa, hey? You okay?*" he hollered out, jumping down the whole second-floor stairway, "*Sosa!*" he yelled again when he got no reply.

When he reached the landing near the kitchen Jimmy J looked down another set of stairs that led to a game room and pointed the assault rifle. He didn't hear a sound which did nothing but piss him off. Jimmy J continued to descend the stairs quietly and cautiously. When he finally reached the concrete, he saw *her* standing in the middle of the game room looking his way. At her side were the dogs he'd heard earlier and behind him laid Sosa in a pool of his own blood.

"*You bitch, you're dead!*" Jimmy J snapped, raising the AR-15 and pointing it at her.

The dogs stood and started growling viciously, the hairs on their backs standing straight up.

"*Give me the diamonds or I'll shoot your fucking tits off, bitch!*" he screamed like a maniac.

She started smirking at him, and said, "You are an idiot," then she laughed at him.

"*Dumb? Nitch I'm not the one with an AR point at my face, you fucking cunt,*" he screeched as he got ready to pull the trigger.

Just as he put his eye to capture her in the sight of the scope mounted on his AR Jimmy J felt the barrel of a gun touch his right temple.

"But you *are* the one with a Glock .40 pointed at yo' dome," he heard a man say.

"Whoa, whoa, whoa. Take it easy, eh? I'm just here to get back 'dose diamonds for my boss. Nobody else needs to die tonight, bro."

With the dogs trotting next to her, the woman walked up to him and took his AR, then she took a step back and pointed his own gun at his face. The man that had been ducked off in the dark recessed section at the bottom of the stairway stepped out of the cut, revealing himself.

Jimmy J saw it was the man that he'd seen eating the girl's ass before he and Sosa came blasting their way into the house. He muttered a curse under his breath, salty as hell that the tables had been turned.

"Who's your boss?" Eric questioned the hit man, standing in front of him, still pointing his .40 caliber at his face, "because from what I've learned, Barry the Diamond Man is dead."

Bunz waited to hear who could still be calling shots. She felt like it had to be another one of the mobsters that might have been in business with Barry. LaLa and Deuce were still at her side, quiet, but ready to rip the intruder to shreds the minute they got the command.

The hit man stayed silent, locked in a stare-down with Eric.

"Got nothin' to say, huh?" Eric chuckled.

"What I'm gonna do, is complete my mission," the man finally said, then as fast as he could he tried to reach back and grab the gun that was in his rear waistline.

"*Get 'im,*" Eric exclaimed to his dogs.

LaLa and Deuce launched from where they were and were on the shooter in a millisecond like they'd been shot out of a cannon. He hadn't even been able to bring the gun around before Deuce chomped down on his arm and bit down as hard as he could. LaLa jumped and chomped down on his crotch, crushing his balls.

The man's blood-curdling screams of agony didn't faze either one of them. Even when he fell backwards to the floor and the dogs' bit, chewed, and ripped at him, Eric and Bunz watched as the bullies did their job. They didn't even wince when LaLa literally ripped the hit man's crotch out. Deuce tugged and yanked until he ripped the guy's arm right out of the socket.

Blood spewed from the man's crotch and where his arm once was. He almost looked like a human fire hydrant in the moment. Deuce finally put him out of his misery by delivering a crushing bite to his throat. He pulled until he held the man's Adam's apple in his mouth before eating it down.

The blood continued to pour our of his body while the two lovers just stood there staring. It was like they were stuck, rooted to the spot by the thought that they had come so close to going to the upper room themselves.

One moment passed and then another and then Bunz was sobbing. Eric just pulled her body to his and rubbed her back as the dogs came back over. They would need a bath since both of them were covered in blood. But that was so far from either of their minds at the moment.

"I shouldn't have come here," Bunz sobbed into his chest, "I'm so sorry, E. I need to leave. However they found me, they can follow me away from you, so you'll be safe. I can't allow you to get hurt or killed because of something *I* did."

She attempted to take a step away to go pack her things and go, but Eric held her hand, stopping her. She turned and looked at him, puzzled as to why he wasn't letting her go.

"You told me you were leavin' me again, Monique," he told her, looking at her with soft eyes even though his words were hard.

"Eric! I robbed and killed a wealthy Italian gangster! Even in death, he's coming for me! It's too dangerous for me to be around you!" she damn near whispered through the tears.

He looked at her, still unfazed by what he already figured would happen by letting her back into his life. He had made that decision even after she had told him everything and he was going to stick with it.

"Mo-Mo, I already knew what I was getting' into when I let you into my house. I know who Barry was," he spoke softly like he would scare her off otherwise.

"Okay, E, so you see why I have to get out of here! I can't bring my problems to you and fuck up all the things you got going on!"

"Monique!" he snapped, needing her to take a deep breath and chill, "I don't think you understand the true nature of what I do for a living yet, so lemme' remind you." He gently pulled her close to him and looked down into her teary eyes, "*I* am the problem solver. *I* solve problems, *little* ones and *big* ones. If my woman has a problem, then *I* take her problems and I *solve* them. *Period.*"

Bunz heard every single word he said, spoken with true passion, very clearly, but what had her heart swelling in her chest and singing at the same time, was how he had just referred to her as *his* woman.

"E… y-you… you called me your woman," she managed to say.

He nodded his head, "I did. I'm a Scorpio, Monique. I go after what I want, and I'm real bullheaded about it. I want *you* in my life, baby… forever."

"Wh-What… what are you sayin' right now, E?" she asked, her voice full of emotion that threatened to spill over.

He looked at the two dead men in his basement, then back at her.

"Right now, what I'm sayin' is I want you to get your stuff; grab *everything*; we're leaving here. There will be more to come so it's best to go somewhere where they'll never be able to go to without the U.S. Army behind them."

Bunz wished that his response matched what she'd had in her head. She had been hoping for the one thing all women wanted from the person they loved most in the world. But that dream would have to wait because he was right. The needed to move and they needed to move fast.

"Okay, baby," Bunz said, understanding that Eric was locked in with her, all too willingly and wasn't letting her go, "thank you, E. For real. I don't deserve you or your love, but one day, I *will*."

Eric couldn't help but to smile at how serious Bunz sounded. It meant a lot to him, to know that Bunz was all in, like he was. He had his ride or die chick back, and now more than ever, he was confident that she was there to stay.

Chapter 10

She got her diamonds out of the safe, grabbed her gun, and packed her bags as fast as possible. With Deuce in the room guarding her, Bunz felt safer than if she had six guns, but she moved like her ass was on fire regardless. Once she had everything that she owned in a couple bags she headed down to the kitchen, where Eric was waiting for her.

"Yeah. There's two of these bitch ass crackers, fam. My front window was blown out, and I'm pretty sure that this car that's in the driveway of where the Bermans lived belongs to these chumps."

Half a minute later, Eric concluded the call and looked at her for a minute. She asked if everything was alright, and he just shook his head. She wasn't sure if that was a yes or a no, but she didn't press further.

"You don't have a phone, right?" he asked, not remembering ever seeing her with one since she'd been back.

"No."

"Did you use a debit or credit card at any of the stops you made on the way here?"

She shook her head. "Cash only. I don't even have a bank account, no I.D., nor a driver's license, E."

Eric got to thinking real hard then. Bunz saw the way his eyebrows had furrowed and grew very concerned.

She walked up to him and put her arms around him. "Talk to me. Please. What are you thinking?"

"They tracked you here, obviously. I'm tryna figure out *how*, though."

Bunz felt her heart drop. She hadn't once thought about being tracked. She figured that how Ernie had figured her out by whatever description was put out by Barry's people, was the only thing anyone knew of her.

Suddenly, Eric's eyes went wide as if he'd just figured it out.

"Monique... pull the diamonds out," he demanded, with a look of revelation on his face.

She hurried to do as he said. Eric put the necklace on the counter and inspected it very closely. Less than a minute later, she saw the change in his facial expression. He waved her to him and pointed to a tiny chip fixed to the back of one of the links. It was so small that even if someone was looking at the back of the necklace, it would never be noticed.

"That's a GPS tracker; it's not completely uncommon to put somethin' like that on high-price jewelry. It's like a tracking device on an expensive car," Eric told her.

While Bunz mentally kicked her own ass for not knowing that, Eric went and got a steak knife and plucked the little chip off. With the hilt of the knife, he crushed the tracker, killing whoever was tracking its way to find Bunz.

"Now, the odds have been evened out," Eric told her. "And *now*, we have the advantage of hunting them, when I holla at my globe trotter. Let's get goin', my brave beautiful problem-solvin' queen."

He grabbed her bags and led the love-struck Bunz and the dogs out to the Escalade. Once they were situated, he hopped in and drove them back to the first home he'd known. It was the one place that no one would dare to go get them... if they knew better.

***

2 Weeks Later

In the heart of *Terror Town*, a south side Chicago neighborhood, for the past fourteen days, Eric and Bunz had made the upper level of a building at the corner of 79th and E. Essex their home. It Across from it was an old lot with a ratty chain-link fence that barely stood up around the whole space.

Eric was born and raised in that neighborhood. He had friends and family there. It was home to a very strong Black community, protected by powerful men that embraced Allah, many of whom pledged allegiance to an organization where men and women, raised up their right hands, closed them into fists, and brought them down to their chest.

Eric knew that the hood was protected by forces stronger than the Chicago Police department. *Nobody* was dumb enough to step into *any* hood in Chiraq that wasn't from there. Not the police, and *definitely* not any individuals seeking to collect a bounty bestowed upon a young woman's head, even if it was because she'd offed an Italian mobster and had taken millions from him. Eric and Bunz were as safe as President Biden in the White House. Maybe even safer.

***

"Sssssssss... Mmmmhm... Eric! Shit, baby!"

Bunz moaned out his name as she arched her back up off the bed. Her legs were spread wide open, her sheer black pantyhose was around her ankles, thong to the side, and Eric's face buried deep in between her legs, dining on her succulent box. He sucked on her clit, doing what he did best to alleviate her of her nervousness about the up-and-coming business meeting that was to take place in just under an hour.

Dressed in a custom crème-colored Ferragamo suit, with the shoes to match, fresh cornrows in his head, and a fresh beard lining, Eric was looking like he was a multi-millionaire business mogul. He'd gotten out his most expensive jewelry for the event that was going to set Bunz up for the rest of her life.

Bunz had dressed in a long suede dress that was the color of wine. It had a tear-drop shaped opening in the center of her chest, long see-through sleeves, and a hem that reached down to her ankles. It fit her curvaceous body like a second skin.

On her feet she wore matching ankle-strapped stilettos with pointed toes, jeweled straps, and shiny gold heels. Her hair was wrapped up in a ball on top of her head. Her eyelids and lips matched the color of her dress. She looked as elegant as an African queen, smelled like candy and he just couldn't resist getting a taste of her before they headed out.

Slurping and sucking on her, Eric brought his woman to a powerful climax minutes later. She squirted in his face, crying out in bliss as she erupted. Eric licked her all the way clean, then as he rose up from in between her thick thighs, he looked down into her eyes.

"Feel better, baby?" he asked her.

She smiled shyly and nodded her head. "I do. I see what Beyoncé means now," she said, giggling as she remembered seeing the world-famous singer on '*Entertainment Tonight!*' reveal that when she gets nervous before a performance, sex helps her.

Eric laughed, "Glad I could help. There's no need to be nervous, though, Mo-Mo. I'm with you."

"I know, bae. It's just… it doesn't seem… real."

"Oh, it will when you see all them Big Faces," he said with a smirk on his handsome face.

Eric took her hand and pulled her up. He assisted her in fixing her clothes then he stepped back and looked at her. He shook his head, truly amazed by her.

"You are the epitome of Black perfection, Monique," he told her.

Bunz heart leapt at his words, "Oh, my God, Eric. You're gonna make me cry, man."

Eric chuckled, "Naw, don't cry. It's a happy day, love." He kissed her lips, then with a cheerful smile, he held out his elbow for her, "may I escort my beautiful Black queen to the chariot that awaits her outside?"

She nodded, "yes, you may, kind, handsome, Black king of mines."

Exiting out of their little bedroom, LaLa and Deuce hopped up from where they were laying in the middle of the living room floor, in a patch of sunlight. They ran to Eric and Bunz, tails wagging, snorting and grunting happily. Eric patted their heads as Bunz grabbed her big leather tote bag, then she kissed both of them on their noses, before Eric led her out of the building, out to where a brand-new executive-edition Cadillac Escalade sat parked, with an armed chauffer holding the door, and a group of armed men standing by as security.

***

The driver piloted the lavish SUV that was built like a luxurious private jet inside, south on 79th. Eyes were on the vehicle the entire ride down to 79th and Vernon, where the restaurant/they were going to was.

The car came to a stop outside of *Josephine's Southern Cooking* and parked along the side of a Hummer H2. Framed between two of the Hummer H2s was a rare white Maybach Landaulet and posted up outside were men in suits, looking like the secret service.

Bunz started feeling nervous again. What Eric had told her about who they were about to meet, she hoped that she could make a good impression and that how she had acquired the diamonds wouldn't matter. After all she was essentially being introduced as a thief.

The chauffer got out and came to open the door. He took Bunz's hand and helped her out, then Eric got out behind her. The men in suits all nodded at him since they knew him personally. That knowledge allowed him to pass through without being searched or anything else.

When they entered the first thing that they noticed was that it was just them and the people they came to meet inside. The restaurant owner had been paid handsomely to allow this meeting to happen uninterrupted.

"Wow!" exclaimed Bunz, as she took in the stylish décor of the place, "this place is beautiful, E!"

"It's dope as fuck, right?" Eric agreed, holding her hand, "the food here is so good that you'll never want to touch a Big Mac or a Baconator again."

She chuckled as he led her to where the banquet hall section was. Bunz saw more men in suits placed around the area. Then inside the banquet hall, sitting at a table by herself, she saw an amazingly beautiful woman there. She was fair-skinned Persian woman, with long silky raven hair pinned up in a style that made her look like she was going to a ball. She was wearing a business suit with a short skirt and heels. The diamond earrings she had dangling from her ears sparkled like the ones in her necklace, on her wrists, and on her fingers. She smiled when she saw them coming.

"Eric," the woman said, standing up out of her chair to greet him and his woman, "it's good to see you again, big bro."

"Hey, Sonia," he replied, giving the much shorter woman a hug and a kiss on her cheek, "been a long time. This is my woman, Monique. She is the lady who has what you'd like to see."

Sonia smiled warmly a Bunz and extended her hand out to her. "Hi, Monique. I'm Sonia; Eric and I grew up together and he's like a brother to me. You're a lucky woman to have locked a guy like him down."

Bunz smiled, looking at Eric with admiration in her eyes. She could agree with her on that.

"Thank you, Sonia. It's nice to meet you and thank you for seeing us."

Sonia nodded her head, "Please. Sit. May I order either of you anything right now?"

"For the moment, we're good. I just ate," Eric said, with a sneaky smile on his face that made Bunz laugh.

Sonia shook her head, smiling herself, knowing how big a freak her play brother was. Bunz sat her bag on the table and was about to sit, when Eric told her he'd be right outside.

"Wait, what do you mean? Why are you leaving me?" she asked, looking at him.

"I'm not. I'll be right outside the hall, baby. This is *your* meeting," he told her.

"No," she stated as she back up, "it's our meeting, E. You and me, or nothing."

Sonia smiled at the two. She had a lot of respect for women who refused to travel through life without the man she loved at her side.

"Eric, please, sit and join us," Sonya requested of him.

He nodded his head, then sat down with his woman. Once he was settled in and she was sure he wasn't going anywhere Bunz pulled out the vintage necklace and the colorful diamonds.

"Wow. Those are some *very* exquisite stones," Sonia said, as she dug into her Birkin bag and pulled out her *jeweler's eye* to inspect the diamonds.

She thoroughly inspected every single diamond looking for flaws or signs that they could be fake. Once she was satisfied with her inspection, she placed her "eye" and the jewels down on the table and took a moment to just look at the couple before her. They were on the edge of their seats waiting for what she had to say to them.

"So. You're the one that took out Barry, huh?" she asked sounding impressed.

Bunz's eyes went wide, and her heart started racing like a Red Eye Hellcat. Her nerves were right back to being on edge when Eric reached out and took her hand, gently cupping it in his.

"Relax, baby. Sonia is *not* an enemy," he assured her.

Bunz looked at him and saw the reassurance in his eyes as well. She trusted him and if he said Sonia was okay, she would have to trust that too.

"I understand your apprehension," Sonia said to Bunz, "you don't know me from a can of paint, but I swear to you, to *me*, Barry was a filthy piece of shit. He was a dirty pig and a creep. He used people as steppingstones to get to where he was, instead of building himself up like a true businessman. Believe me, Monique, if it hadn't been *you* that got him, many others were gearing up to do it. They just probably couldn't have done it single handedly."

Bunz relaxed a little as Sonia spoke.

"I never did business with him personally, but diamonds I've bought and/or sold has gone through his hands. He did indeed have the connection to some very expensive stones but know this; you need not worry about me. Eric is my brother, and you are his woman."

Bunz nodded her head in understanding. "It was… either him, or me," she said, then ran down a brief recollection of everything that led up to that bloody night.

Sonia leaned back in her seat. "You are a brave woman. I respect your gangster all the way. Just to let you know, the necklace is beyond what I think you've probably figured it was worth, and colored diamonds like these are very precious and hard to find. I am prepared to offer you $165 million dollars for all of them, right now, all cash."

Bunz's jaw dropped. "$165 *million*?"

Eric was shocked at that number,

"Yes," Sonia nodded, "to be honest, they're worth a little more, but I need to make a profit, and they'll be a little difficult to sanitize."

Bunz looked over at Eric. The look on his face told her he felt just like her.

"What do you think?" she asked, looking to him for guidance.

"It's not up to me, Mo-Mo," he told her, "I'm only here to support you."

"And to help carry all the heavy money," Sonia chuckled.

Bunz took a few deep breaths to calm her nerves. She looked at Sonia and nodded her head.

"I'll take it."

Sonia nodded her head. She looked at the bodyguard that was closest to her and gave him a nod. He pulled out a little 2-Way radio and called to one of his men in the crew. Seconds later, three men carrying extra-large plastic cases entered the banquet hall. They brought the cases to Bunz side and left out.

"Please check the bags so that I can know if you are satisfied," Sonia requested.

Bunz opened one; she saw so many brand-new big faces inside of it. She had never seen that kind of money in her entire life. The knowledge pushed her to open the next one and the third. All the money looking back at her made her feel like her body was on overload. All this money was hers and she just couldn't process it.

$165 million dollars! I have $165 million fucking dollars! I am rich! she thought to herself, so close to having a meltdown.

"You okay?" asked Eric, reaching over to take her hand into his.

Bunz was lost for words. She was nearly paralyzed with shock.

"I think she's experiencing what some would call shellshock, Eric," Sonia said, picking up a manila folder that was on the seat next to her, "I have something else for you two, though; this is the information you requested. I hope this helps you."

Eric took the folder and opened it while Bunz peeked over his shoulder. As he went through the pictures and documents, he explained to her what they were looking at. Bunz looked back up at the beautiful diamond connoisseur in front of her.

"He told me you had a big problem on your hands, Monique," she said with a smile on her pretty face. Then she looked over at Eric, "Can I say it?"

He chuckled, then nodded his head.

Sonia looked at Bunz, then she quoted Eric's motto, "*Problem solved!*"

All three of them burst out into laughter. Sonia had always loved when he said that and now, she had gotten her turn.

"Know this, though," she added, "the only way to completely handle this problem, Monique, Eric, is to *kill 'em all*! *Nobody* lives, or they *will* come for you one day."

Her words turned the laughter into silence. The importance of what she said was well received by the two of them. Everyone linked to Barry the Diamond Man's inner circle, at some point, had to die.

"But, for the moment, let's eat; I ordered a smorgasbord for us," Sonia told them then she called out for the food to be brought out.

The food came and they dug into the delicious cuisine, savoring the taste of *real* southern cooking.

***

"Thank you again, Sonia. I really appreciate you," Eric said, as he and Bunz prepared to go, stuffed from the delicious plates of southern cuisine.

"No problem. Take care, you two," she replied, shaking Bunz's hand, then she hugged Eric, "and I will be doing my best to assist you as well."

Eric nodded appreciatively. "Cool. Keep me posted."

Two of Sonia's men assisted Bunz and Eric with her newfound wealth, carrying the cases of cash out to the Escalade. Sonia watched them all leave out. Once the door was shut, she got her iPhone out and made a call.

"Yeah?" answered a man.

"Tell your boss that I have the diamonds. I want *$200 million* for them, or you will *not* get the diamonds, nor what your boss really wants."

"One moment."

Sonia waited, listening to chatter in the background. He could hear the boss talking. A second later, he was back talking to her.

"Where are they?" he asked.

Sonia laughed. "You must think I'm Boo-Boo the fool. When I have my money, then you'll get your info."

In an instant, Sonia's phone vibrated against her face. She looked at the screen and saw a notification, for a deposit in the amount of how much she requested in her private Swiss bank account.

"Thank you. I will send you their location via GPS coordinates now. I make only this suggestion, though," Sonia said, "wait before you do anything; they've got a lot of protection, and where they're staying, you will not get in and out without many casualties. Let them stew, lose sleep; psychological warfare is one of the best methods of torture."

"Uh huh."

The call ended without anything more. Sonia smiled to herself, then sat back down. She reached for her champagne glass, smiling, chuckling to herself. She took a sip of the Dom, then held the flute up.

"Problem solved, Sonia. Good job, girl," she told herself, then got up to take her leave.

Chapter 11

"Ooooohhhh *shhhhheeeeeeiiiiiiiiit*! Damn, baby! Fuck! You tryna make a nigga's toes break off!" Eric groaned.

His eyes rolled to the back of his head, as Bunz deep-throated the shit out of his dick. On her knees with his pants and boxer briefs down at his ankles, she was going hard to please him while the Escalade rolled. His hardness throbbed in her mouth while she used one hand to jerk while she sucked. She released his cock and spit on it before making eye contact with him. She took her time telling him all the dirty shit that was on her min while coating him in the mix of pre-cum and saliva. When she felt like she had talked enough she took him back into her mouth damn near inhaling his dick like a porn star whose rent was due.

"*Fuuuuuuuuuuuuuuuuuck*!" Eric roared, his toes curling up so hard in his shoes that he felt like he'd bust up out of them.

She took his dick to the back of her throat, sticking her tongue out so that the tip of his dick could touch that lil' dangling thing at the back. She giggled with it down her throat, making him jump when he felt the vibration in his balls.

Eric leaned his head back and enjoyed her way of showing how much she truly appreciated him turning her into a multi-millionaire in just an hour's time. Bunz spit his dick back out a second later, dying to feel him inside of her. With a mischievous grin, she got up, turned around, and pulled her dress up. Eric's eyes went as wide as dinner plates when he saw all that panty-hosed ass in his face. He reached forward and kissed her ass, then he ripped a big hole in the ass section.

Bunz slid her thong to the side and lowered herself down on his dick. Eric's heart rate sped up as his arousal grew tenfold. The sight of her fatty bouncing up and down on his length, and the feeling of her wetness was enough to make him bust his nut in just under ten minutes.

Bunz hopped off when she felt his dick pulsating inside of her. His grunts and groaning told her he was there, so she dropped back to her knees and sucked his dick until he exploded in her mouth, filling it all the way up with globs of semen.

She stroked and sucked until he was empty, and her mouth was all the way full. She swallowed it all, savoring his taste and licking him clean, followed by her lips.

"*Mmmmhm*, E you taste so good to me baby," she purred, getting up to fix her dress.

"I got plenty more for you when we get back home, love," he told her, pulling her to him so that she was sitting on his lap.

She smiled and kissed his forehead. "Can't wait. Maybe we can fuck on a million dollars, huh? How's that sound?"

"Like a muthafuckin' dream come true."

They both chuckled.

They arrived at their apartment minutes later. The group that had been there when they left, were there to make sure they got inside safely, and stayed safe. Eric had made it a point to hire a huge team of men and women that were willing to die to protect his woman.

The chauffer opened her door and held her hand as she got out. Eric got out behind her; he helped with the money cases, entering their spot to be greeted by an excited LaLa and Deuce.

"I'll be right to you, my queen," Eric said, as all the money was stacked up in the bedroom, "I'ma let the dogs out in the back."

"E," she called to him, as he turned to leave out.

Eric stopped in the entryway and looked at her. Bunz dropped her dress on the floor where she stood, then she scooted onto the bed, giving the Playboy magazine pose, with a knee up and that sultry sexy look on her face that made Eric want to pounce on her right then and there.

Eric smiled, then he looked up towards the ceiling at where a skylight window gave a view to the dark sky.

"Thank you, God, for giving me a queen and a freak at the same time! You *are* the man!" he said, then hurried to take the dogs out, so he could get back and dig his lady out.

***

The Following Night

In the parking lot of a big the strip club in Joliet, Mane, a dark-skinned dread head, groaned in bliss as the thick honey-gold complexioned chick deep-throated his dick. He was leaned back behind the wheel of his brand-new Bentley truck, sitting up on chromed 24" Forgiatos. He had the woman's tiny, leather Rag & Bone skirt raised up over her hips, his middle finger in her asshole, finger-fucking it the way he was planning to do with his dick.

Her gold, blue, and white Versace top had been tossed in the back seat, along with her LaPerla lace bra top. Her plump 34-D cup breasts were free, nipples erect. On her feet still, were her gold 6" Red Bottom stilettos.

As she kneeled on her knees in the passenger seat, hunched over the center console with her ass tooted up high, the girl's head bobbed up and down in his lap. She moaned as she sucked and slurped, going crazy. The amount of cocaine she'd just snorted that Mane had given to her, had her lit like a Christmas tree.

Mane's eyes rolled to the back of his head as she started sucking harder and faster. Yo Gotti and E40's *Law* bumped from his audio system as Mane continued thrusting his finger in and out of her anus, dying for the chance to put his dick inside of it.

The girl released his cock and ran her tongue down to his balls. She licked all over them before sucking them both into her mouth. With one hand, she gripped his shaft and slowly jerked him while she sucked on his nuts.

The honey-gold beauty was going *hard* to earn them dollars. Mane met this girl at the club every Friday night to see her shake all that ass and make it rain on her. Every night that she worked, before she left, she met him out in the lot, hopped into whatever whip he pulled up in, and orally pleased him to fatten her money bag up. Mane utilized the love she had for the white powder.

It fueled her to do *all* the nasty things he wanted her to do without any hesitation. Mane was her best customer, but not the only one she had. The girl was so gorgeous and thick that all of the ballers around the way frequently came to see her shake her ass, and to have the chance to have her put it on them. They all paid top dollar for her explicit extracurricular services, but unbeknownst to them, she had a secret that could get every single one of them jammed up.

Mane groaned loudly as he reached his hand around to her rear end. "Damn, Amanda! *Fuuuck!*" the rich heroin dealer cursed, taking his finger out of her ass and smacking on it. He swore the girl was trying to suck his soul out of him, "yeah, bitch! You workin' for it tonight! *Shit!* Get this money, shortie!"

Amanda used one of her hands to start jerking him while she sucked, knowing that would get him there faster. She had more dicks to please after Mane. Time was of the essence in her world.

Mane started bucking and kicking. His toes started going crazy in his Gucci loafers. As he felt his nuts tighten up, his

PROBLEM SOLVED

back arched up. Amanda tasted his pre-cum and gripped him tighter and sucked even faster. Seconds later he exploded in her mouth, roaring like a wild animal.

She kept on jerking and sucking him, until her mouth was filled with his essence. She put on a show for him by spitting it all back out on his shaft, then she slurped it all back up, swallowing it all up, pretending she was on camera, auditioning for a spot on *Porn Hub*.

"Mmmmm, damn Mane. You taste so good!" Amanda said, purring at him, wagging his softening dick like it was a dog's tail. She rose up in the seat, turning herself towards him, letting her breasts catch his eye, "did you like that?"

"Hell yeah! You's a beast! I'm tryna crack, though, shortie. Lemme' hit that fat ass from the back," Jimbo told her, with his dick still out. "All that ass you got, a nigga damn near gon' get cho' ass pregnant and take you up outta the club scene."

Amanda giggled, "I hear that. So, you don't give a fuck that I'm only 16 years old, and you're 28?"

"Hell naw! Who gon' tell? Not me," Mane stated, as he reached for her hand to pull her over to him. "Yo' lil' young ass look grown anyways. That fake I.D. got you shakin' ass here, so believe me, ain't nobody questionin' you at all, and ain't nobody crazy enough to question *me*."

Amanda allowed him to get her onto his lap. She straddled him, letting her dripping wet pussy rest on top of his dick. In a matter of seconds, she could feel him getting hard again.

"Damn, nigga, yo' dick must be battery-powered or somethin'," she said with a laugh.

"My dick stays hard for a bad bitch like you. I'm tryna tell you, shortie. Fuck this club shit; come fuck wit' a real nigga like me. You see how I'm ridin'. Who the fuck else round here ridin' a Bentley truck? These broke-ass niggas out here ain't on shit. They cop from *me! I'm* the man! *Me!*"

Amanda chuckled, "I hear that, baby. I might be able to make somethin' happen, but right now, I need you to stop talkin' and lemme' ride this dick."

She lifted up a little, reaching under herself to grab his hardness. Sliding her pussy over him, she penetrated herself, moaning from how thick and long his dick was. It made her want to bite him, from how much he filled her up. Even though he was just a dollar sign to her, she *did* like fucking him.

Amanda rode his dick, gyrating her hips, bouncing up and down as the sound of EST Gee *Love is Blind* featuring 42 Dugg came from the speakers.

Mane groaned and cursed as the pussy overpowered him. She had that wet-wet that a nigga would kill for. She rode him until she climaxed all over his dick, then Mane tossed her into the back seat, jumped back there with her and got behind her as she tooted it up for him again.

He grabbed her ass cheeks, parted them, and spit a wad of saliva down onto her ass hole. His dick throbbed like it had its own heartbeat as the sight of her puckered asshole excited him. He put the tip of his dick to it, smeared his spit around it, then he started easing into her.

Amanda moaned as his size stretched her out. It hurt her, but it felt good to her at the same time. She gritted her teeth and took it like a champ. With money on her mind, all pain and pleasure were welcome.

Mane fucked her asshole, watching his dick go in and out of it. He held her cheeks open, excited by the sight of it and by the sounds of her moaning and screaming. He loved the idea of dominating a bad bitch like Amanda. Making her submit to him. He got off so easily on it, especially when it was a chick that was too young and dumb to realize that he just wanted to fuck her.

When he felt his nut coming, he pulled his dick out and started jerking it. He aimed the tip at her backdoor, then seconds, later, he exploded. He skeeted inside of her crack, dropping his load all over her asshole.

"Wooo!" he shouted, feeling so satisfied, "Maaan, oh muthafuckin' man! I love this fat juicy booty, shortie!"

Amanda giggled and made her ass wiggle for him. Mane smacked it, watching it jiggle like it was filled with Jell-O.

"Aight, Mane. I gotta go, baby," she told him, lifting herself up.

"You mean you gotta go see another nigga," he surmised, feeling his ego deflate.

"Hey, I'm gettin' this money off these *pay-for-play*-ass niggas," she told him, keeping it real with him, as she sat up to fix her skirt. "Don't worry about nobody else, though. Don't nobody else got a spot in my heart like you do, Mane."

"Bitch, I don't give a fuck about you' heart! All I care about is that mouth, that pussy, and that ass!" he told her.

Amanda frowned. "Well fine, then. Fuck it, since all you give a shit about is fuckin', go find you another bitch to do that with," she told him, then went to reach in the back to get her bra and her shirt.

Mane shot his hands out and grabbed her tracks, yanking her to him. She screamed as pain exploded in her scalp.

"Bitch, you got me fucked up if you think you and I are done!" he told her.

"*Let me go, mane! You're hurting me!*" she told him.

With all his might, Mane yanked her forward and slammed her face into the glove compartment. She cried in pain. He did it again, and again, until she was knocked out.

Mane started his engine and was about to put it in drive, when a black Ford F-150 pick-up truck pulled up in front of his Bentayga and stopped.

"Man, what the fuck?! *Move the fuck outta the way, clown!*" he shouted.

Beeping the horn, he started revving his engine up. He couldn't see inside the vehicle. The windows were tinted, and it was too dark outside.

Mane put it back in park and opened his door to go make the driver move. The second his foot touched the pavement...

WHAM!

A hard blow from behind instantly sent him face down on the ground.

***

Eric held the miniature wooden bat as he looked down at the knocked-out dope boy. Bunz had already hurried over to check on the young girl. On stand-by, LaLa and Deuce stood on security, watching Bunz's back while she gently leaned the girl back.

Eric grabbed the man with one hand and dragged him towards the stolen pick-up truck. Bunz lightly patted the girl's face until she came to. The girl immediately started freaking out, eyes going wide with shock when she saw the strange woman's face, with the two big dogs behind her.

"Hey, hey, hey, it's okay! Relax! I'm not gonna hurt you!" Bunz told her, with her hands on the girl's shoulders, "you're gonna be okay! Chill!"

The young chick took a few deep breaths and calmed herself down. She looked out the windshield and saw a man with braids toss what looked like Mane, tied up, into the bed of the pick-up truck that had stopped in front of them.

"What... what happened?" she asked Bunz.

"You were about to experience something that *no* woman, young or old, should ever be subject to. For now, though, I'm getting you up outta here."

Bunz quickly helped the girl get her clothes back on. Eric called out to LaLa while Deuce stayed with Bunz and got into the Bentley truck with her and the young chick. Bunz pulled off behind him, riding past a few people on the way to enter the club, totally oblivious to what had just happened moments ago.

***

"She's one of my homeboy's nieces, bae. Take her to her mother's crib. I'm sendin' you the address now," she heard Eric say through the SUV's speakers.

Following behind him up I-55 towards Chicago, Bunz cruised the Bentayga at the speed limit. She had learned the young girl's name and introduced herself and Deuce to her.

"Got it. What about you, though?" Bunz asked, looking at LaLa sitting in the pick-up's bed, standing guard over the tied-up would-be rapist.

"Oh, *believe* me, I'm good. I'm takin' dude swimming," Eric told her, "Take the SUV to my mans up in Nogo. I'll send you the address. He'll have another whip for you that's clean."

"Okay, E. Be safe please."

"You, too, beautiful."

Bunz ended the call and sighed. She glanced over at Amanda and saw that she had turned around and was patting Deuce's head. He licked at her, attempting to give her doggie kisses. Bunz smiled but she still felt bad. The girl was so young, doing what most grown women shouldn't even be doing.

"Amanda," she called to her.

Amanda looked at her.

"When I drop you off, I'm gonna give you my number. If you are ever in need, call me," Bunz told her.

Amanda nodded her head. "Th-Thank you… um…?"

"My name is Monique, but most people call me Bunz."

"Okay. Thank you, Bunz."

An hour later, Bunz got to Amanda's mother's house up in North Chicago. She turned into the driveway and pulled up to where Amanda's mother stood at the door. It was like the situation with Nikko; it saddened her that so many young kids were being used, abused, and led astray. Bunz made it a mental note, that from that moment forward, any young girl in need of help, whether they wanted it or not, she was going to be there for them. Period.

***

Mane pissed his pants when he woke up and saw the huge dog standing there. The dog growled viciously, baring her sharp teeth. He scooted away from her. She remained where she stood, but her eyes were locked on him.

He could tell he was outside. The sky was pitch black. Not a star was up there. A noise got his attention. He looked down by his feet and saw the tailgate door of what he realized was that of a pick-up truck was lowered down.

"Who the fuck are you, fam?" he questioned, "and why the fuck am I tied up?!"

"I'm the nigga that's gon' teach yo' bitch ass a lesson for puttin' yo' dick inside of young girls and then beatin' them up like they owe you somethin'."

Mane yelped as he was yanked out of the pick-up's bed. He hit the ground hard, landing with a thud that knocked the air out of his lungs. Dazed, he heard the man call to the dog. She jumped out of the bed and took her place next to him.

"Fam, come on, joe! Why you trippin' about a lil' thot ass bitch?" Mane asked incredulously, as the man grabbed a set of thick chains from the cab of the Ford. He was met with silence. Then before he knew it his legs were being wrapped in the chains.

"Aye, man! What the fuck is you doin'?" Mane demanded, growing more afraid by the second.

"I already told you, bitch ass nigga," the guy told him, "I'ma teach you a lesson, one you will never forget."

Mane watched him put a lock on the chains that bound his legs. With his arms tied with plastic zip-ties, he could do nothing but attempt to wiggle away.

"Bruh, come on, man! Please! Lemme' go, joe! Shortie just a lost little bitch, fam!"

WHAM!

The man kicked Mane hard in his jaw, knocking the whole front row of his teeth out.

"You got kids, homie?" the guy inquired.

Mane shook his head, "No!"

"Well, that *lost little bitch*, is someone's daughter. If you had a little girl and she came across some lame-ass nigga that uses young girls when he should step his game up to get a grown woman, what would *you* do?"

Mane looked up at him. He had no reply.

"Exactly. You ain't gotta worry about havin' no kids now, though, home boy," he said, then he grabbed the end of the chain and hooked it to the pick-up's trailer hitch.

***

Eric called LaLa and hopped into the F-150 behind her. He put it in drive and rolled forward. The man screamed as he was dragged on the asphalt surface of the big, deserted beach parking lot. Eric rolled the window up and turned the music on. He looked in his mirror at the man. Doing ten big circles, Eric dragged him around until he was sure that plenty of skin had been left behind.

He put it in park and got back out with LaLa behind him. He walked back to the guy and saw how horrible he looked.

The guy trembled and shook. Skin had been scraped from his face and his arms. He looked like someone had taken a potato peeler to him.

"Does it hurt?" Eric asked.

He looked at him. His mouth bled profusely. He attempted to talk, but the agonizing pain was too much.

"It's okay. You ain't gotta tell me; I know it hurts, because you ain't the first clown I dragged behind me, and you will not be the last."

Eric then pulled out his Glock and cocked it. He pointed it at the man's face.

The guy tried to plead for mercy. *"Wait!"*

BOCKA!

"Shut the fuck up! God forgives, but I do *not*! Rest in piss, bitch ass nigga!" he told the dead man.

Pulling out the burner phone he brought with him Eric dialed the number to his homeboy and waited for the answer.

"What up?" the man answered, sounding like he was ready to hear some good news.

"Problem solved, my man. No charge," Eric said, then ended the call.

Chapter 12

One Month Later

Bunz and Eric spent the month building their empire, one day at a time. Everything she wanted to do he made happen. While they were building, they were still out there solving people's problems whenever they were needed.

She got very interested in real estate, so he assisted her in finding cheap houses and apartments to buy, fix up, and then flipped them for a profit. It went so well for her that she bought double what she had before and hired a team of décor designers to assist her in making her turn an even bigger profit.

For Eric, Bunz surprised him with his own weight-lifting gym, which doubled as a dog strength-training facility, for those that had dogs that were tough.

They moved out of the Terror Town apartment and bought a penthouse loft in a high-rise in the heart of Chicago. Living in the lap of luxury was like nothing they ever truly ever expected to have at any point of their lives. They were chauffeured around in exclusive executive-edition SUVs, and whenever they felt like tearing the highways up, they hopped into one of their exotic cars and embarrassed everyone they could.

Bunz even invested a few million into Eric's main business. He had a connect that made a personal trip in from the Dominican Republic to deliver more cocaine than he had ever seen in his life. Eric quickly became the man you wanted to see for Grade A cocaine, whether you lived in Illinois, or around it.

Life was good, business was good, and money was making money. Nothing could be better than that.

***

Upon returning from a trip, they had taken out to Athens, Greece, Eric got a call from another of his regular clients in need of his services.

"He needs to learn how to keep his muhfuckin' hands to himself. I'd do it myself, but he called the cops on me once already, you feel me, fam?" the guy said.

"Indeed. I'm on it, bruh," Eric told him, then the call was ended.

"Duty calls?" Bunz asked, lying next to him in their humongous platform bed, in their expansive bedroom, with the dogs laid out with them.

"Yes, ma'am," Eric smiled at his beautiful queen, "I will be back to y'all *asap*," he told her, placing a hand on her belly, rubbing where their child was growing. "Maaaan, I cannot *wait* 'til my little one gets here. I *still* can't believe that I'm finna be a father."

"For real, right? We gon' be the dopest parents ever, bae," Bunz told him, excited to be pregnant by the love of her life.

"Lemme' go make us this money, beautiful." Eric looked at the information about the target that had been sent to him, by another phone. "This one is gon' be fun."

Bunz watched him get up and go into the closet and gear up. When he came out, he had his book bag, and the keys to his *punishment* mobile.

"Make *sure* you come back to me, E. Remember what we promised each other," Bunz said to him.

He nodded. "I'll never forget that Mo-Mo. Always come back to each other, no matter what happens."

He went and planted a soft kiss on her forehead, then patted the dogs' heads and headed out.

Bunz phone rang minutes after he left out. It was a random number, but she answered it anyways.

"Heya, toots. I bet you think that because you're in a relationship with a hit man, that you're safe, eh?"

Bunz frowned when she heard the person speak with a voice distorter, sounding like Darth Vader.

"I'm still alive, ain't I, bitch?" Bunz replied, curling her lip up. "Fuck you hidin' yo' voice for? You scared to say who this is? And why the fuck y'all keep on calling me? Fuck the talkin', joe. Catch me in traffic, *pussy*."

The voice laughed. "For a pregnant bitch that used to live off swallowing cock, you sure talk a *lot* of shit. When I catch you, I'm gonna let all my guys give you a real run for your money. I can't wait to see how many dicks can fit inside of you at one time."

Bunz chuckled. "I hear you talkin', still, but I ain't seein' shit, bitch."

"You will. Trust me, whore. You're gonna start losin' sleep after this one. Just know this: I am *untouchable*; the world is *mine!*"

The call ended, leaving Bunz seeing red. For a second, she looked at the blank screen of her phone, then she shook her head.

"Whatever, bitch. Come see me like a real gangsta. All that talkin' ain't 'bout shit. Bitchass cracker," she said to herself, then she put her phone to the side and got back to watching her movie.

***

"Bitch, what the fuck I tell you about back talkin' me? I said get cho ass in there and cook a nigga some food, I'm hungry!" the brutishly huge man with a thick beard and a

very bad anger problem yelled at the woman in front of her three young children.

Carla fought back tears as she thought about how this wasn't the first time he had snapped at her like this. It was like he didn't appreciate shit that she did for him. He was living in her house, with her kids, while she worked all day to put food on the table. It didn't matter to him that her feet were sore from the heels she had worn at work all day. Or the fact that she had *just* walked in the house all of five minutes ago.

"Jerry!" she snapped back finally having had enough of his shit, "stop yelling and cursing! I don't want my kids hearing that stuff!"

WHAM!

Jerry hauled off and punched her in her jaw. He hit her so hard that she went flying into the wall behind her. Dazed from the blow, Carla started sinking down to the floor. Her kids heard the commotion, and the three little girls came running to their mother's side. They stood in front of her like little bodyguards while she sat on the floor crying her eyes out.

"*Stop it! Don't you hit our mommy anymore!*" Carla's oldest daughter, Penny, yelled at Jerry, standing up to him with no fear in her heart.

"*Shut up, you little bitch you ain't my fucking child,*" Jerry roared, then he swatted her hard enough that she fell against her mother.

The other two tried to block their big sister and their mother, using their own bodies but it was pointless. Jerry reached around them and snatched Carla up by her hair.

"*I said cook me some fucking food before I break yo muthafuckin' neck bitch!*" he spat before he damn near threw her towards the kitchen, not caring about shit she had going on.

BAM! BAM! BAM!

Jerry's rant was interrupted when someone started pounding on the door. He grew even angrier at whoever had the audacity to knock on *his* door like that. It was enough for him to leave Carla alone in that moment and storm over to the door. He didn't even bother to look into the peephole before he yanked it open, ready for a war.

"Special delivery, my man."

Jerry saw the tall braided-up man in the Pizza Hut uniform, holding a burgundy pizza box heat-case holder in his hands.

"Ain't nobody order no muhfuckin' pizza!" He turned to where Carla was being helped up by her kids. *"Bitch did you order a fucking pizza so yo lazy ass ain't have to cook?"* he demanded as he turned towards Carla.

"No!" she cried, staggering to her feet, ready to run if necessary.

"Aye, my man. She ain't order this, fam," he heard the pizza man say.

"Then why the fuck are you here?" Jerry snapped, turning back around.

The second he spun back around to the man, there was no longer a pizza heat case in his hands, but a high voltage taser.

"Her baby daddy sent me, bitch ass nigga," the guy said, then he squeezed the trigger, and popped the woman-beating punk.

Carla ran to get her daughters as Jerry hit the floor, shaking and convulsing from the powerful shock. Pulling the three of them to her and holding them close, shielding them from what was happening in front of them, Carla looked at the man in the Pizza Hit uniform. She had heard him tell Jerry that her baby daddy had sent him. Carla wanted to kiss her children's father so badly at that moment.

Seconds after immobilizing the guy, the man in the uniform stopped tazing Jerry and looked at her.

113

"Take the kids to their room and stay with them for a minute. This man will *never* harm you or your children again," he said to her.

Not knowing exactly what to say, Carla nodded her head before starting to direct the girls to the back of the house while he dragged the giant man out of her house.

"Mommy? Who was that man?" her youngest, Tee-Tee asked, in the tiniest voice that Carla loved so much.

"He's a pizza delivery man, baby," Carla told her, kissing her forehead, "you all stay in here until I come get you. I'll be back," she told them all.

Closing the door, Carla hurried out of the room, wincing from the pulsating pain in her jaw. She ran to the big window in the living room and looked out. She was just able to get a glimpse of Jerry being dragged into the back of a windowless van.

"Make him cry like a bitch, whoever you are," she said to herself, happy as hell to finally be free of the abusive asshole.

***

Out in a deserted area in Chicago, along Lake Michigan, Eric looked down at the woman-beater. He had the big man butt-naked, his wrists bound with duct tape, his ankles shackled with chains that were hooked to the back of his van. Thinking about his words from handling Mane, Eric chuckled to himself.

The big old industrial area was so desolate, that even if someone screamed at the tops of their lungs… *nobody* would hear them. That was the big reason why he loved bring people out to die here. He'd always seen that crooked cop Hank Voight on *Chicago PD* bring people out her to take them out. Now he did it too.

Jerry pleaded for mercy, begging Eric to spare him. Eric looked at him like the man was crazy.

"Are you serious right now?" Eric asked incredulously. "You abuse a woman *and* her kids, which *aren't* yours, when you're *supposed* to protect them."

"*I'm sorry bro! I swear I'll never do it again! Please,*" Jerry sobbed.

"Oh, this I know, my man," Eric said, then went to hop back into his van.

He started the engine, put it in drive, and slowly pulled off, looking in his mirror. Through his open window, he could hear Jerry's blood-curdling screams as he was dragged behind the van. The skin on his back was being shredded and peeled off by the dirt and rocky ground.

Eric turned the music up, blasting DJ Drama's *Smoke* featuring Gucci Mane, Willie The Kid, and Lonnie Mac as he dragged Jerry around in circles. After he did four, headlights appeared, coming from where the entrance to the area was. Eric did another circle as he saw the '87 G-Body Monte Carlo SS riding up and pausing. He drove over by it and parked, hopping out to greet the man who had contacted him for the job.

The man behind the wheel heard the cries of the man who had beat on his baby mama and their children.

"You're just in time for the show, my dude," Eric told the guy.

"Please proceed," the guy said, cutting off his engine and grabbing his blunt of exotic weed to puff while he watched.

Eric went to the back of his van, opened the doors. Jerry started pleading with him again. He needed this shit to stop. His back was pouring blood like a faucet since all the skin had been burned off by the asphalt. Eric heard him but instead of untying him he grabbed a bottle of clear liquid and took it over to Jerry.

"*What is that? Come on man, please,*" Jerry started begging. If he stopped for a minute, he would see the irony since Carla had begged him the exact same way plenty of times before.

The man in the SS got out, puffing his loud. Jerry heard him walk up. He gasped in shock when he saw Carla's baby daddy there.

"Sean, bro, tell dude to let me go! Come on fam, help me out!" Jerry damn near cried thinking he might be saved.

Sean looked at him with a raised eyebrow. "Nigga, you out cho' muthafuckin' mind." He looked at Eric. "Whatever that shit is, *please* make it hurt this bitch ass nigga as much as possible."

Eric smirked evilly. "Say less," he said, then he started squirting the liquid all over Jerry, making sure he got a lot of it on his back.

Jerry screamed so high-pitched that Eric and Sean had to plug their ears with their fingers. The concoction of grinded-up Ghost Peppers, lemon juice, and salt burned him like fire. Jerry flopped around like a fish out of water. While he tried to pull against the chains that held him where he was, Eric went to get the *finalizer* from the back of his van, while Sean kept puffing his loud, watching revenge take place.

With a razor-sharp machete, Eric stepped back to Jerry. Jerry saw the cutter and cried like a little girl, so terrified that he shit on himself. He begged and pleaded both Sean and Eric. Both men ignored him letting him cry until Eric got tired of it. Moving quickly, Eric raised the machete high over his head before swinging it hard and fast, separating his right arm from the rest of his body. He mimicked the cut on the other side and blood spewed from the stumps. Not quite done with him Eric picked up one of the arms and got in Jerry's face with it.

"Nobody likes a guy that hits woman," he told the screaming man.

SMACK!

With Jerry's own hand, Eric smacked the shit out of him in his face.

"You's a *bitch*," Eric told him.

SMACK!

"And so is yo' daddy for not teachin' you better."

SMACK!

"And now, you *die!*"

Eric tossed the arm to the side. He raised the machete up high over his head, then silenced Jerry forever when he brought it down as hard as he could, slicing right through the center of his face.

Jerry died on impact.

Eric looked at his client. "Problem solved, my brother."

Sean nodded, then walked to his Chevy. From the back seat, he got a bag of cash and went to give it to Eric.

"There's the $10,000 for the job, and there's the $20,000 I owe for the two bricks you hit me with last week."

"That's what I'm talkin' about, fam. Good look," Eric said, taking the bag and tossing it into the back of his van.

"I'll be callin' you soon, bruh. I been havin' some issues with some clown-ass niggas comin' 'round my neck of the woods, tryna start forest fires 'n shit."

"I'll be glad to put the flames out if they get too hectic for you," Eric said, dapping him up.

Sean nodded his head, then hopping into his SS, he left off, leaving Eric to clean up.

Eric got a can of gas and bleach he had mixed before he placed Jerry's arms over his chest, poured the flammable liquid all over him, and then lit the deceased pervert on fire. With a bottle of ammonia and bleach, he cleaned off his machete while the corpse burned. Once he heard sizzling like bacon, Eric hopped into his van and pulled off, ready to get back home to his woman.

Chapter 13

Bunz was at the elevator door when it dinged along with Lala and Deuce waiting for Eric to finally make it home. When the elevator opened, she nearly ran to him, throwing herself into his arms, hugging and kissing him like it'd been years, again, that she hadn't seen him.

"Well, damn!" Eric chuckled at how she was all over him. "Did I do somethin' to deserve such a warm emphatic welcome?"

She didn't respond, instead burying her fast in his chest holding on to him like a lifeline. He quickly realized that she was sobbing, shaking, and trembling.

"Monique? Hey?" He pulled back a little so he could see her face. He saw the tears in her eyes. "What happened?"

She told him about the call from the guy, threatening her and he was *heated*. He started seeing red, feeling his blood boil.

"It's gon' be aight, baby. You are surrounded by killers and there's not a soul that could get into this building without getting' popped. The security systems are high-tech, and you got two killer XXL Bullies that'll die for you. Relax. Take a deep breath for me, please?"

She did as instructed and took a deep breath holding it for a second before exhaling. He had her repeat the process until she was able to speak without crying.

"Does she really know what she's doing, E?" she asked him, with his arms wrapped around her, "we have a whole lot to lose if she fumbles this."

"There is no fumbling with her, Mo-Mo. We *win*; we do *not* lose," he told her.

His optimism made her feel more confident. She smiled, wiping away the tears that had rolled down her face. She was about to speak when Eric's business phone rang again.

"Goddammit!" he cursed, pulling it from his pocket. "One sec, bae," he told Bunz, then answered the call, "speak on it."

"I need a problem solved. Are you available?" asked a woman.

"Depends."

The lady spoke cautiously. She told him about her husband, a criminal defense attorney that had been skimming money from her inheritance, which her deceased father had left for her. She wanted to get even with him and only knew one way to make that happen.

"Okay. I can help you," he replied still looking at Bunz, enamored by the raw beauty that she couldn't possibly realize that she had.

"First, I need you to come to my home. I have things here that can help influence what crime scene personnel will conclude."

"Shoot me the location and I'm in route."

He ended the call and saw Bunz was now looking away from him. He could already tell that she didn't want him to go.

"I won't be long," he told her.

Bunz nodded her head. She wanted to ask him to stay but couldn't bring herself to do so. He'd been solving problems for people since before she returned to his life.

"I love you, E," she told him instead.

"And I love *you*, my queen," he reciprocated.

With that, Eric went and got his tool bag, changed into all black sweats with a hoodie, and got the keys to his 2007 Suzuki Hayabusa 1300. He kissed his woman, patted the dogs, then hurried out to go make some more money. He had plans to turn his business line off afterwards for an entire day. The next move he had was going to be *big*, and it would be his most grand one ever.

***

On his powerful crotch-rocket Eric sped from Chicago up to an area called Vernon Hills. He followed directions being spoken to him through his Bluetooth earpiece and ended up in a deluxe neighborhood not far from the big shopping mall Vernon Hills was known for.

Cruising along the dark quiet street, Eric purposely went past the woman's house, getting a good look around, scoping out anything that sent up red flags. As he'd rolled past, he saw through the large living room window, a woman in the living room, doing aerobics work out in front of a huge TV screen. He bent the corner and found parking near a man-made pond and made his way to the woman's house.

***

Goddamn! This bitch bad as fuck! Fuck type of clown would do a chick like her wrong? Eric wondered to himself, when the gorgeous woman answered the door.

Her hair was ink-black, her skin was Mediterranean brown; she had an exotic look that made Eric think she was Greek or something close to it. On top of that her body was *cold*. She wore bright green Fabletics workout apparel that was lightly soaked with sweat from her hard-core work out. Her exposed upper chest area glistened with sweat beads that ran down into mouth-watering breasts. Her lips had Eric's attention; he was sure they'd been plumped with filler, but

120

he found himself still envisioning how they'd feel wrapped around his dick.

"Hey," she said, way more flirtatiously than what Eric expected, "thanks for coming on such short notice. Come on inside."

She stepped back, allowing him into her lavish home. Eric stepped inside and looked around, nodding his head in approval. The whole bottom floor was laid out like a celebrity's mansion. She was living *real* good. No wonder she was trying to knock off her husband for fucking with *her* money.

He looked at her hand and saw that she wasn't wearing a wedding ring.

"By the way, my name's Anastasia. What do I call you?"

"The problem solver," he told her. "What do you have to show me?" Eric asked, as the woman licked her lips seductively, gazing up at him, with eyes full of liquid desire, and lust.

"Follow me," she nearly purred to him.

She turned on her Air Jordan cross-trainer sneakers and led Eric towards a custom stairway that led to the upper loft level. His eyes went a straight to her perky little ass as she walked ahead of him.

Boooooy, whoever created Fabletics knew how to make ass look sooooo muthafuckin' good! Eric thought, as her ass hypnotized him.

The woman led him to her big bedroom. Inside, she opened a drawer and pulled out a file with documents in it, then she showed him the contents of one of her husband's drawers. Eric was amazed that a woman that beautiful could be that vicious. It made him chuckle, because his woman was a monster, if made to be.

"You really wanna' do this?" Eric checked, knowing that often, people reacted out of anger, not taking a second to think that regret and guilt was as deadly as actually killing someone.

"He's robbing me of what *my* fucking father left for *me*! My father was *killed*! I want what is *mine*, and the *last* person that should be taking it is my own damn husband! *Fuck him!*" Anastasia cursed angrily.

Eric was convinced that she was sure.

"Okay. You do know that you will be the number one suspect when the police come sniffing around, right?"

"Yes. I do. Let *me* worry about the pigs," she told him.

"He's at the office now?"

"Yes. He'll be there until 10:30, with his little bitch. Before you go, I have another problem I'd like you to solve for me, Mr. Problem Solver."

Eric looked at her with a puzzled expression. "And what might that be?"

She started smiling then. "I've been very horny, for a very long time, and there's nothing I'd love more right now than for you to drop those sweats and let me suck that big Black cock before I fuck all over it. Can you help me with that, Mr. Problem Solver?"

She stepped closer to Eric, closing the gap between them. Her breasts touched his sternum. Her hand grabbed his crotch and felt his throbbing hardness through his sweatpants.

"I have a woman," he told her, trying *sooooo* hard to resist.

"And I have a husband, but what they don't know won't hurt them, right?" she asked, digging her hand down into his pants, gripping his wood and going wide-eyed when she felt how big it was. "Wooow… it really is true what they say?"

Eric started laughing. "What? That Black men are the ones with the biggest dicks?"

"No," she said, dropping his sweats and boxer briefs, freeing his length. Looking up at him, she said, "bad bitches like *me*, get what I want, *when* I want it," she told him, then she sank down to her knees and opened her mouth wide.

Eric's toes curled as the beautiful woman took him into her mouth. It was so warm. The sight of her juicy lips wrapping around his dick was what he'd visualized when he first glanced at them.

She deep throated him like a pro, taking him to the back of her throat, not gagging at all. She grabbed his shaft with two hands and twist-stroked it while she sucked his dick. Eric cursed and gutturally groaned. She was going crazy on him.

Thank you, dumbass husband of hers! he thought to himself, as Anastasia moaned while she sucked.

A minute later, she spit his dick out and stood up. She turned on her Jordans, walked towards her bed, and pulled her tight spandex work-out leggings down. Eric's dick got even harder when he saw she had neither panties nor a thong on.

She bent over, looking at him. He waddled over to her, pants still around his ankles. Getting right behind her, he grabbed his cock and positioned himself at her opening. He slid inside and felt like he'd just gone to a whole other world of pleasure.

She was so hot and wet and tight. Eric's eyes rolled to the back of his head as he pounded her. She cried out and moaned, loving how thick he felt inside of her. She leaned her face down on the bed and begged him to make her cum.

Eric gripped her hips, gritted his teeth, and went savage on her. It took just eight minutes for her to cum. She exploded all over his dick.

He pulled out of her, tossed her onto the bed. She pulled her bra-top off, freeing her little breasts, then kicking her shoes off, she pulled her leggings off and flung them. She laid on her back and pulled him to her. Eric got between her legs as she put them up in the air. He slid back into her wet-wet and hooked her legs over his shoulder. He then started jack-hammering her, pounding her relentlessly for ten more minutes, until she climaxed again.

Eric got her back onto her knees and stuffed his dick back into her mouth. She sucked and jerked his cock until he busted his nut, filling her mouth up with hot semen. She kept on sucking and jerking until he was all the way empty, then she let it dribble out of her mouth, onto her chest.

"Mmmmhm," she purred, licking her lips clean of his jizz, "I love how you taste, Mr. Problem Solver. I'd love for us to be able to do this again."

"It's possible. For now, though, I have a job to do. By the way, I need half up front," Eric told her, as he pulled her up, then fixed his clothes.

"No problem," she told him, then naked with her breasts covered with his cum, she sauntered off, switching her ass, entering a large walk-in closet.

She came out a few minutes later, with three large rubber-banded stacks of cash, handing it to him.

"It's all there; $15,000 cash, handsome," she said, before her lips curled up into a smile. "I'll be seeing you very soon after this."

"Sounds good," Eric told her, tucking the cash in his hoodie pocket. "I'll let you know when it's done."

With that, he left the horny married woman and headed back to his bike, go get on business.

***

"What the fuck you mean, you got *robbed*, dude?! Y'all muhfuckas got shooters all around and you let a nigga get out on y'all?" snapped Bunz, when one of the men from one of her and Eric's trap houses called to inform her that they'd just taken a significant loss.

"Come on, Bunz, chill. It was a guy posin' as a cluck. I let him come in to get served and he pulled out a Draco. We ain't really have a choice but to let him get what he wanted. I won't even cap; we was lackin', but on 'erythang I love, we gon' catch him."

"I'm on the way. Y'all niggas better not leave before I get there, or y'all all finna laid it down!" Bunz declared, then she ended the call.

"LaLa! Deuce! Let's go! We got shit to do!" she yelled out.

The dogs came running. Bunz got the key fob to her limited-edition Maybach Mercedes-Benz G650 4x4 Squared Landaulet, grabbed her big Chanel tote bag with her FN tucked inside of it and led the dogs out to the underground garage, where her drop-top G-Wagen sat parked.

***

"Alonzo, are you ready to leave yet? My feet are so sore, and I am starving!" Jane told him, as she sat on the long leather couch across from his desk, rubbing her pantyhosed foot.

"In a second, dear," Alonzo told her, as he counted the stacks of cash that had just been dropped off by the mother of a client's child. "Hey. Could you go and-"

KNOCK! KNOCK! KNOCK!

Alonzo stopped talking mid-sentence and looked at the door, then back at the young blonde chick he'd been fucking since he'd hired her.

"I thought Selena left?" he asked.

"She did."

Alonzo's eyebrows furrowed. "Then who the hell is in my office? How'd they get through my main door?"

"I don't know, babe. I was in the bathroom."

Grumbling under his breath, Alonzo got up and went to open the door while Jane sat quietly on the couch, not a fan of his anger at all.

He got to the door and unlocked it. He turned the knob, opened the door, and…

CRACK!

A wooden baseball with barbwire wrapped around the business end bat flew right into his forehead, splitting it open. The blow killed Alonzo on impact. His body flew backwards and hit the hardwood floor with a thump.

Jane jumped out of her seat and screamed. She saw the masked man that had just killed her boss, stepping into the office, with the bloody spiked bat. She was so terrified that her bowels loosened, evacuating so much that it pushed out of her panties, into her pantyhose and started running down the insides of her thighs.

Eric's lip curled in disgust as he smelled the foul odor permeating the air inside the office. He saw brown liquid dripping from under her little skirt, pooling around her high heels.

"P-Please! D-D-Don't kill m-meeee," she begged, crying her eyes out.

"I won't hurt you. Get me a bag and put all the money in this office inside of it, then I will leave you," Eric told her.

Jane hopped right to it. She waddled to where Alonzo's briefcase laid on his desk, threw the money that he was counting inside, then retrieved every dollar he had stashed around inside. She even took the Rolex off his wrist in tossed it in.

Slamming it shut, she handed it to Eric.

"That's everything! I swear!" she promised him.

"Good job."

He pulled out a silenced Sig Sauer and pointed it at her. She screamed, scooting back against the wall, trying to shield herself with her hands.

"*No wait! You promised you wouldn't hurt me and you'd leave me alone if I did what you said! Please,*" she sobbed.

"This *won't* hurt, and I *am* gonna leave you," Eric said, then squeezed the trigger three times.

PFFT! PFFT! PFFT!

He shot her in the center of her. Her brains exploded out of the back of her head, splattering all over the wall behind her. Her body dropped to the floor and blood started pooling out.

"Stinking," Eric then added, looking at the twitching corpse.

Eric then dug into the front pocket of his hoodie and pulled out the half kilo of cocaine he'd brought. He put it inside the top drawer of Alonzo's desk. Upon suggestion from Anastasia, he was to make it look like an angry drug-dealer client of his had come for revenge. It was told to him that several times, Alonzo had been accused of accepting drugs as payment and indulged heavily.

Eric put a little coke on top of the desk, made some lines, then he smeared some under Alonzo's nose, and Jane's nose. Eric then got up out of there, unseen, unheard, hopping back onto his crotch-rocket that he had parked a couple of blocks away from the office building the crooked attorney's office was.

Getting to his Hayabusa, Eric hopped on and started the engine. Before he kicked it into gear to ride off, he sent a text to Anastasia.

Problem solved; he typed then hit send.

Just before he put his phone back into his pocket, he got a text message from his woman. He read it and cursed under his breath. Pocketing it, Eric put the kickstand up, kicked it into gear, he peeled off in a rush to get there to assist his woman.

Chapter 14

Bunz whipped her G-Wagen into the alley way that ran behind the Hebron apartments, where she and Eric had dope spots in each of the seven buildings there. The crowds of dope boys and dope girls knew the Mercedes truck well and got the hell out of her way as she yanked it to the left and parked at the building she was going to.

She jumped out with her tote bag, LaLa, and Deuce. All the hustlers and gangsters that were outside knew something was up. They'd all gotten wind of the robbery from earlier and knew there would be some serious repercussions. Eric did not take loses, and neither did his woman.

Bunz stomped through the two buildings until she came to the door the stash spot was behind. She barged right in, startling the six guys inside, whom were all smoking loud and drinking, while two were playing a game on the PlayStation 5.

The leader of the spot, a tall lanky 22-year-old dread head called Mug, dropped the blunt of Kush in his lap, burning his Balmain jeans when Bunz burst through the door with the big dogs behind her.

"Oh shit… Bunz," he said, in a state of shock.

"So, this is what the fuck y'all doin' after a nigga dun' got out on y'all muthafuckas?" she snapped, slamming the door shut behind her, "playin' fuckin' games 'n shit when y'all *should* be out findin' that bitch ass nigga?!"

One of Mug's newer guys, called Benzo, that hadn't met Bunz yet, smacked his lips and waved her off. Bunz head snapped to look at him like he had lost his mind.

"Nigga, I *knooooow* yo' bitch ass ain't just wave me off like I'm a muthafuckin' peon!" she yelled, digging into her tote bag and pulling her pistol out.

"Oh, whoa whoa whooaa!" Benzo panicked, hopping up from the chair he'd been sitting in. "Shortie, chill out, joe! It ain't that serious!"

The others gasped.

"Shortie?" Bunz asked, with a raised eyebrow.

"Oooooo... bruh... you just called the boss's lady a shortie," said Pipes, one of Mug's other guys.

Benzo swallowed hard as Bunz raised her gun up and pointed it at him.

"W-Wait a minute! I meant-"

BOCKA!

Bunz put a 5.7 x 28 mm round right in Benzo's dick. He screamed louder than a woman in labor without an epidural, hitting the ground and gripping his bleeding crotch. The others froze in fear since they knew how she got down. Add the fact that she was a G, to her being the boss's woman, they didn't want those types of problems.

"Anybody else wanna' lose their reproductive organs for callin' me a shortie?" Bunz asked, waving the gun around at them.

They all panicked, trying to jump out of the way.

"Bunz come on, boss lady! We don't want no problems with you!" Mug proclaimed, rising from his chair, hands raised up to display he wasn't on shit.

LaLa and Deuce stepped forward, growling, with their eyes locked on him.

"That's dog-talk for sit cho' bitch ass back down, dick head! And if you get up again, I'ma shoot cho' muhfuckin' dick off and let my bitch eat it!" Bunz told him, pointing her gun at him.

Mug plopped right back down just as the door flew open. All the young guys nearly pooped their pants when they saw Eric enter, with a big-ass Desert Eagle in his hand.

***

Eric quickly assessed the situation inside of his spot. He saw Mug's guy Benzo on the ground, bleeding through his crotch, and his woman, with her FN Five-seven in her hand and his dogs standing at her side like they were supposed to do. The others looked scared shitless.

"Anybody care to explain why my pregnant woman had to come down here and shoot some dumbass little nigga in the dick? I know she ain't do it because she's bored," Eric said to them all.

He stepped up to her, placed a kiss on her cheek, then waited for an answer, which didn't come fast enough for him.

"Deuce! *Kill!*" he ordered, pointing at one of Mug's guys at random.

"*Noo, E!*" screamed Nash as Deuce charged at him.

LaLa stood obediently with Bunz as Mug, Beans, Blade, and Rex all watched in horror as Nash was mauled before their very eyes. The big XXL Bully chomped down on his right hand and Nash tried to yank away, but that only made it worse. Deuce crunched down and yanked until his hand broke away from his arm at the forearm.

Nash grabbed the bleeding stump, screaming in pain, as he bled profusely.

BOOM!

Eric squeezed the trigger on his semi-automatic .357, obliterating Nash's head.

He looked at Mug then, turning his gun on him.

"E, hold up, wait a minute, bro!" Mug cried.

BOOM!

A shot to the chest opened him all the way up. Mug flew backwards and hit the wall, sliding down to the floor, dead.

Beans, Blade, and Rex, along with the incapacitated Sticks remained where they were, terrified. They all remembered what had happened to Zip. They knew that Zip had *intentionally* stole from Eric; Mug had just been caught lacking and still wound-up dead.

Eric took a moment and then looked at the man that had been working almost as long as Mug had. Beans started trembling but did his best to not show it.

"You're in charge now, lil' nigga," Eric told him, "Do *not* lose money; that *is* your only warning. Have I made myself clear?"

Beans nodded his head fast. To the others, he spoke again. "Y'all get these bitch ass nigga cleaned up. Now!"

"Wh-What about B-Benzo, E?" asked Rex. "He gon' n-need a doctor, fam."

BOCKA!

Bunz put on in the center of Benzo's eyes, rocking him to sleep.

"No, he won't," she then said.

Eric looked at the remaining three. "People would kill for the spot you're in. People will also die if I come up short. I'm *not* fuckin' playin' with none of y'all niggas, joe!"

"On 'erythang, E! I swear, big homie! I got you. No more losses! *None!*" Beans swore.

"I hear you talkin', famo. You got only one chance to show me," he told the man, then he took his woman's hand and escorted her and the dogs out of the spot.

Outside, the group of twenty-three men and women that had been posted up in the alley awaited Eric's word. He looked at them all. They looked like they were hungry.

"Y'all ready to work?" he asked them.

"Yeah!" they all shouted, some of them raising up their guns to the sky.

"Good. This is a takeover. Every-fuckin'-body that's sellin' somethin' around here, they either kick in or they lay down. Fuck sharin'; go get 'em!" he told them all.

Without another word, the mob ran to their whips to go get to hunting the competition. They were ready. Receiving word that Eric was on some everything is his type shit, they were thirsty to prove themselves to him. He was the man, and they wanted to be on with him. Period.

"Let's ride, my beautiful goonstress," he told his lady, once the last vehicle of his shooters dipped off.

Bunz giggled when he gave her juicy ass a smack.

"I wanna go out to eat, bae," she told him as they walked, holding hands to where his crotch-rocket was parked next to her Maybach G-Wagen.

"Say less. Hop yo' thick ass up in the driver's seat and follow me home to drop my bike off, then we can go anywhere you want."

Eric held her hand as Bunz climbed up into the lifted-up SUV. He kissed her on the lips, closed her door, then after he let the dogs into the back, he went and jumped onto his bike.

Bunz started up the big V12 engine under the G-Wagen's hood as he fired up his Hayabusa, put the kickstand up and kicked it in gear. She led the way out of the Hebrons with Eric following behind her heading through Zion, to the highway, where they shot south towards Chicago.

As he followed behind his woman's exclusive SUV, Eric felt his nervous. He was a goon, a gangster, and a killer, through and through, but what he was about to do, was something he had never thought he could do. It had him stuck in his thoughts, wondering *what if...* nearly the whole ride to their penthouse, as the move he was ready to make would affect him for the rest of his life... and hers.

***

Down at MacArthur's, a popular restaurant out west in Chicago, Eric held the door for his woman to enter. The eatery was a spot that everyone came to, even though it looked like a plain jane restaurant in the hood. The broke ate there and so did the rich, folks from the hood, and people from the suburbs. Photos of great people, which included Barack Obama hung around the walls and inside the aroma of real soul food filled the establishment. Bunz's and Eric's mouth watered, and their stomachs growled with hunger. Bunz wondered to herself why she'd never been there before as long as MacArthur's had been there.

After they were seated, they ordered beverages and food. Eric brought up a few things with Bunz about a few investments he'd been wanting to make but waited until they had time to talk about it together. Bunz felt so honored that no matter what he did, she was included in it. It almost brought tears to her eyes from how considerate he was.

She agreed with everything he wanted to do, then she brought up a few suggestions herself. He told her about the magazines he'd been reading, where food trucks were making a comeback in various cities. He also spoke on possibly buying a few car washes, gas stations, and clothing stores, but what interested Bunz most, was his suggestion on getting a few buildings to start assisted-living homes for the elderly.

"I'm with you, baby," Bunz told him, "Every step of the way. I got half on whatever."

Eric smiled and nodded his head. "There's somethin' else I want you with me on, Monique."

"Name it," she told him.

He took a deep breath, then sliding out of his seat, he stepped around to where she sat. Bunz turned her head and looked up at him, slightly puzzled.

"Monique. Baby. I can't even describe the ways that I love you. You truly complete me, my queen."

"Aww! E, you're gonna make me cry! I'm pregnant, man!" she chuckled as her eyes began welling up with tears from his passionate words.

"Naw, baby. Don't cry; this is a night for smiles and happiness," Eric told her.

He then dug into his pocket and pulled out a little cream-colored velvet box.

Bunz's eyes went wide, then, as Eric sank down to one knee, she screamed so loud that everyone in the restaurant looked their way to see what happened.

He opened the box and revealed the flawless 8-carat diamond engagement ring inside. Bunz gasped when she saw it.

"Monique Reese Duque… will you make me *thee* happiest man on earth, *more* than I already am, and marry me?"

"*Yes!*" she screamed. "*Yes! Yes! Yes! Yeeeeessss!*"

The people in the restaurant all clapped and cheered loudly for them. Bunz jumped out of her seat, hopping up and down excitedly as Eric took the ring out of the box and slid it onto her finger.

The fellas whooped and hollered, shouting out props to Eric while all the ladies screamed congratulations to Bunz, geeked to see a beautiful Black couple so in love with each other that they were ready to become one.

Eric stood up once he had officially made Bunz his fiancée. He wrapped his arms around his future-wife and kissed her lips, sealing the deal. Bunz's tears rolled down her eyes as she realized she was experiencing the happiest moment of her life, with the love of her life, in such a great smelling restaurant.

***

After they tore up plates of fried chicken, cheesy macaroni, sweet potatoes and greens Eric took his woman back to their spot and made love to her repeatedly, until the sun came up. When they got up, he cooked for her and after he massaged her whole body with hot oils. He pampered his queen, going hard to show her that she meant the world to him.

In between their alone time, he took a few business calls, then together, they saw on the news, that reports of *Vicious murders of drug-dealers around Lake County, Illinois* had cops baffled and people tripping all over, scared to death to sell a dime sack of weed. The reporter spoke on how this large group of killers were kicking in the doors of known drug houses, killing everyone inside, taking everything of value, then burning everything to the ground.

Grinning at their goons, Eric and Bunz delved back into each other, fucking each other's brains out as every single one of their businesses thrived and made them tons of money, every hour of the day, without them even having to leave their bed.

***

3 MONTHS LATER

Sitting on a couch that was mounted to the custom-made deck, Eric and his woman were taking in the beautiful early morning sunrise together. The dogs sunbathed in a big patch of sunlight in the middle of the roof-top. Bunz was reading an Urban Fiction novel that he had told her about cuddled up next to him. It enticed her enough to purchase it online. After she read the first three chapters of *Raised By A Goon* by Ghost she was hooked. When she looked at the publication company that the writer was with, **Lock Down Publications**, she looked at the website and saw so many other urban fiction stories, written by so many other talented writers, all of them from the hood with street experience and mindsets.

She even saw that the owner was a man that had done nearly 30 years in prison, creating the company from inside the joint. Eric had told her how dope it was to know that a person in the most fucked up situation can establish something so prestigious and was selfless enough to lend a hand to others that had dynamic stories to tell.

Eric chuckled, glancing over at his woman. She was so into the book that her eyes were as wide as one watching a horror movie, dying to know what happens next. At that moment his phone started ringing just then. He glanced over and saw his homie Macho was calling.

Answering the call, Eric enthusiastically shouted, *"Yeeeooo!"* as the *Steel City Mafia* was known to always shout.

"My nigga, I apologize for the interruption, but *yoooo*, I could *really* use ya help if you can lend a hand," Macho stated.

Eric could hear the urgency in his guy's voice. Something was clearly wrong. Macho had never been the type to lose his head, so this made him sit straight up.

"Talk to me, bro. Everything aight, fam?"

"No. Everything is *not* okay. I need your help, like right now, cutty."

"Say less, my nig'. I got you. Lay it out for me," Eric told him, ready to boot up and get going.

Chapter 15

Bruno chuckled as he watched the two female truck drivers struggle to get free. With tape over their mouths, and tied to steel chairs, the women couldn't move nor talk. Off to the side of the massive section of the building they were all in was an industrial-size rock crusher machine that was used to crush boulders and turn them into gravel.

At Bruno's side was his right-hand man, Charlie, who oversaw the city-sized rock quarry. Originally from Moscow, Bruno and Charlie had come to the United States using money they had made doing wet work for the Russian mafia to start their own thing. Choosing Schaumburg, Illinois to plant their feet, since it was one of the biggest crime ridden states, filled with rich people wanting to get rid of other rich people, Bruno and Charlie had been making *tons* of money, murdering anyone with a *very* high price on their head.

The two had been in the Russian military for years back in Moscow before getting in bed with the Russian mob. Bruno, formerly a General in the military, was reputed to be the Russian version of Fidel Castro. He was a murderous son of a bitch with no conscience. Charlie was a monster, but Bruno was a demon who had no morals.

Before they left Russia Bruno had assembled a team of heartless killers, that he and Charlie had been in the military with, to come and make money by spilling blood wherever they were paid to do it at. They all had reputations that stretched as far as the sharpest human eye could see.

During a job on a cocaine drug lord, Bruno learned of a big-time cocaine importing family of Dominicans that stemmed from the Dominican Republic and all over the east coast, and out to the Midwest. Bruno brought it to Charlie and the two did their research and learned the men who were in charge were worth billions and were owners of big trucking companies that transported heavy machinery and other specialized types of freight. They were brothers and one was said to be a die-hard goon, who went above and beyond to protect his people.

Immediately, Charlie came up with the idea to get the company owners to cough up what he and Bruno wanted. They ordered two new construction machines, reached out to the company owner to hire his trucking company to pick their new machines up and deliver them to their quarry. Right after the two beautiful ladies that had pulled up in the fancy semi-trucks carrying their pricey new front-end loaders, off-loaded the new Caterpillars Bruno and Charlie snatched the girls up and tied them up.

The call had been made to ransom the women's freedom. 100 kilos of the pure Dominican cocaine that they had been hearing about for quite a while now, or the two ladies get pulverized.

* * *

"You do not scare me, in case you are thinking you do," Bruno said to the ladies with a thick Russian accent, as they both mean-mugged him, "but what you should fear, is if your boss does not cough up the cocaine. I hear that he has plenty of it, so your lives should be well worth losing a few dollars. What do you think, ladies?"

The taller more robust one with red hair and high-yellow skin muttered something that Bruno knew was her saying, "*Fuck you, bitch.*"

The other chick, who had skin the color of dark-chocolate, and dread locks, remained quiet, but stared at Bruno with fire in her eyes.

He and Charlie chuckled.

"These girls are tough, Bruno," Charlie said, "let us see how tough they are if their boss doesn't deliver."

Bruno looked at the Patek Philippe on his wrist. "Your boss now has just 30 minutes left to save you," he told them, then his eyes went to the red head.

Taken by her, Bruno walked towards her. He reached his hand out and squeezed her right breast. The girl jerked away and muttered more curse words.

Always having been the type to love being fought by women, Bruno bit his bottom lip. The fantasy he'd had in his head when he first saw the statuesque woman get out of her truck re-played in his head. Bruno had never once had sex with a woman of color. He planned to change that before he killed the girl.

"Hmmmm… I hear that Black pussy is the best," he told her, moving his hand down to between her legs, "maybe I should find out before I put you and your friend into the crusher, no? What do you think about that?" he asked her.

The darker chick started flipping out as the Russian's hand slid down into her friend's pants. The red head tried to squeeze her legs shut to keep his fingers out of her.

He laughed at her, ignoring her protest and he pushed his hand further down into her panties and jammed his finger into her vagina. The girl squealed in panic as his finger violated her. She bucked and kicked as his cold finger penetrated her.

"Bruno," Charlie scolded, disgusted by what he was seeing, "what are you doing?! We are killers, not rapists! Stop that at once!"

Ignoring his right hand, Bruno pushed his finger further up inside of the girl. The girl's eyes filled with tears. She looked up at him and vowed death upon him inside of her head.

"Do not fight me. You know you like this. What is it you people say... *Do not front!*" he told her, then shoved his finger up even *further* and curled it.

She cried in pain as he wrecked her. His jagged fingernail scratched her sensitive walls. She kept trying to curse him out, but the tape muffled her words. The other girl cried for her friend. It was as bad to her as witnessing someone being stabbed to death while being helpless to help them out. It made her want vengeance *so* incredibly bad.

Bruno pulled his finger out of her and saw blood on it. He curled his lip up in disgust. He then wiped his finger off on her forehead. Turning back to Charlie he saw that his comrade was shaking his head in disdain.

"That is sick, Bruno."

Bruno's phone rang just then. He pulled it out and saw he had a video-call. He pressed *accept* and looked at the screen. He saw the face of a man with golden-brown skin, a razor-sharp beard and hairline, with long dread locks. The fire in his bluish-gray eyes burned like a wildfire that could not be extinguished. The man looked *pissed!*

"*Ugaday kto?*" the man said to him.

Bruno's eyebrows furrowed up as he looked at the guy. He didn't look Russian at all. Hearing him speak his language puzzled him.

Glancing over at Charlie, Bruno looked back at the screen and spoke. "I do not wish to '*guess who?*' Who are you?"

"I'm ya' worst nightmare, pussy," the guy said, now smirking at Bruno, "you like snatching women up, huh? That's how you handle business? All just to get my attention and make me come see you?"

Checking out the background, Bruno could tell he was in a vehicle. An oval-shaped emblem in the headrest behind his head had *Peterbilt* embroidered inside of it.

Bruno smirked back at the man, "That is the idea. I assume that you are Mr. Valdez?"

"Assuming only makes an ass out of you, but *not* me," he replied.

"I'll take that as a yes. So, Mr. Valdez, I am Bruno. I have these two lovely ladies who are depending on you to deliver. How long will you be with my merchandise?"

He smirked at Bruno then the camera went to a stunningly beautiful woman with a caramel skin complexion and long silky royal blue hair.

"He doesn't like talking to bitches," she told Bruno.

Bruno got pissed, "You have quite a mouth on you, lady. What else can you do with it?" he asked and started smirking.

"The question you *should* be asking me, is will your body be sent back to Russia so your mother can burry you properly or will she die too for pushing a failure out of her stank-ass pussy?"

The Russian's smirk faded. He grew irate with anger from the insult to his mother. He and the woman locked eyes. She grinned at him, winked, then blew him a kiss.

"*V rossi takiye zhenshchiny, kak vy, rabotayut v publichnykh domakh,*" he told her, saying, "*In Russia, women like you work in whore houses.*"

He grilled her with a venous glare. The woman chuckled at him.

"*V Amerike, ty suka,*" she replied to him, saying, "*In America, you are a bitch,*" then the video-call ended.

Charlie heard the whole thing and tried to keep from laughing at the furious look on his boss's face. Inside his head, though, he *was* laughing his ass off.

141

Bruno cursed. *"Gryaznyye amerikantsy! Ya ub'yu ikh vsekh!"* he declared, cursing all Americans and promising death to them.

***

Two hours went by. The sky went from blue to black within the hour. High-powered lights around the property lit up the entire 5-acre area. Just past a quarter to 9 Bruno and Charlie stepped outside the building onto the long loading dock section. There were nearly fifty armed men outside. All of them on point and waiting for their boss to give them word.

Walking out and taking their perch on the ledge of the dock, Bruno nodded in approval when he saw how ready his men looked. With their Russian-made AK-47s hanging from shoulder straps, back-up pistols inside holsters, extra clips in auxiliary belts, and all of them wearing body-armor they looked like they were ready for war.

They were all dead silent as their two bosses emerged from the building. Trained and acting like a regiment of soldiers from back in the *glory* days, they turned and stood at attention, waiting for them to speak.

Bruno smiled, then nudged his partner with his elbow. "Life is good, no?"

Charlie shrugged. "I would agree, when it comes to prosperity, Bruno, but not foolishness. I do wonder, why exactly are we going about extorting this man, when we have plenty of money to buy wholesale?"

Bruno chuckled. "Where is the fun in that? We do not buy anything from the competition, Charlie. We *take!*"

He looked around his vast property, happy with what he saw. He and Charlie had more than $30 million dollars' worth of heavy-duty machines parked in a row off to the side that his employees used to make their jobs way easier. A few big garages that had been built to keep the expensive equipment in working order sat on the opposite side. The employee lot was filled with the vehicles belonging to the mob of armed men.

The Russian then looked at where the two semi-trucks that the lady truckers pulled onto the property in were parked. He smiled even bigger, thinking about how he was going to fuck the shit out of the red head chick, in front of her boss, then kill her in front of him, then kill him, after he and Charlie got their coke.

Talking with Charlie about some business, Bruno paused mid-sentence when the sounds of a loud truck's engine brake roared out into the air, from very close by. He and Charlie looked around. There were so many tall trees that lined the outside of the perimeter fence, that neither of them could see the road from where they stood. Hearing the truck get closer, the two turned their heads towards where the entrance road was. After watching the entrance, seconds later, Bruno and Charlie saw lights.

A semi turned into the property, pulling a long dump trailer.

"You are expecting another delivery at this time?" Bruno asked Charlie.

He pulled out his iPhone, and went into his schedule app. Looking at it, Charlie frowned in confusion, shaking his head.

"No. There are no trucks scheduled to come here until tomorrow afternoon," he replied, as the tractor-trailer rolled up the path road in their direction, "there must be a late one coming, or the driver could be lost."

As it came into the light, they both saw the creepy old 1985 Peterbilt 359 Extended Hood. The tall lights that lit the property up shined on it perfectly, but the windows were tinted. Neither Bruno nor Charlie could see the driver, not even the driver's shadow.

Most of the trucks that came were bringing stones and boulders that would be crushed and made into various sizes of gravel, so Bruno and Charlie thought nothing of it. There was no company name visible on the truck, nor on the trailer. However, seeing that the old rig was rolling in their direction of where his men stood, instead of the section with mounds and hills of boulders and rocks, where the last trucks of the day had dumped their loads, made both Bruno and Charlie furrow up. Bruno shouted in Russian to one of his men to stop the truck redirect the driver.

He and Charlie watched one of the men walk forward, entering the path that the semi was traveling in. Once it got right alongside the man, the driver of the semi brought the big rig to a stop. Standing about a hundred feet away or so from where the mob stood, Bruno squinted his eyes, trying to catch a glimpse of the driver when the person behind the wheel rolled the window down.

Suddenly, the driver began revving the engine up causing the truck to start shaking like a race car with a powerful engine. Flames shot up high out of the exhaust stacks as the truck continued to shake angrily. Charlie swallowed hard and as he and Bruno watched the truck, he started to develop a *really* bad feeling in the pit of his stomach.

Bruno watched the guy he sent knock on the driver's door. The engine continued revving loudly out of the straight exhaust stacks. Flames continued shooting up into the air. With his hand balled into a fist, the man pounded on the door again. He shouted for the driver to roll the window down.

The window stayed up. He pounded on the door once more, threatening to open the door himself and drag the driver out of the truck if they did not roll the window down. Just then, loud rap music began to play. The bass from the powerful sound-system inside made the ground seem to shake under the Russian's feet.

The man looked back at where Bruno and Charlie stood and shrugged. As he waited for Bruno to tell him something the music got *louder,* and he turned his head back and saw that the window was now rolling down.

He was about to shout to the driver that he was in the wrong section, when the man found himself staring up into the business end of a 12-gauge Mossberg pump shotgun.

His jaw dropped as his eyes went wide in fear. Bruno and Charlie saw it and they both gasped in sheer shock.

The man tried to turn and run, but his efforts were futile.

BOOM!

The driver pulled the trigger, as the man attempted to run. Bruno, Charlie, and the other men watched his head get blown clean off his shoulders. His headless corpse hit the ground. Blood spewed out of the stump, pooling around his body.

"Shoot the truck!" Bruno commanded his men.

He and Charlie saw the remaining forty-nine take aim at the truck, when six masked figures' heads popped up from over the edge of the side wall of the dump trailer, and they were all wielding *big* military-grade machine guns.

"Dear God…" Charlie gasped when they opened fire.

***

Eric, Macho, Tool, Javier, Xavier, and Danny squeezed the triggers on their fully automatic .50 caliber *M249* machine guns, all of them equipped with 200-round boxes. They all swept left and right, spitting so many rounds that the Russians didn't have a chance to even think, let along shoot back. Their body armor did *nothing* to stop the swarms of the huge .50 caliber rounds. The Russians got to flipping and flopping; body parts flew all over the place. Their heads exploded like those of the living dead in the game '*Call of Duty: Black Opps*'. It was gruesome and had Bruno and Charlie close to puking their guts up.

"Shit!" Charlie cursed, panicking as he and his partner watched in horror as their whole team were reduced to piles of bloody meat and tissue.

He and Bruno both took off running, back into the building, leaving their men to get themselves to safety. They ran past where the two ladies were, rushing to get to their office, where they had an emergency exit. They could still hear shooting, but slowly, it was dying down, as were all the blood-curdling screams that came from their men.

Bruno passed Charlie, grabbed the back of his shirt, and he yanked him out of his way slipping past him. Charlie hit the floor hard before skidding into a wall.

Reaching the office, Bruno pushed the glass door in so hard that the glass shattered when it banged against the interior wall. He ran for the exit and pushed his way out, sighing in relief as he made it out, until he saw a man standing there, with a sawed-off shotgun pointed right at him.

Struggling to get up, Charlie cursed Bruno out in Russian. Not hearing anymore shooting, Charlie scrambled to get back up onto his feet. He was about to run inside the office when he was hit *hard* from the side by a massive furry body. He was taken down to the ground.

"*Aaagh! Help me! Help!*" he pleaded as sharp teeth sank into his shoulder damn near to the bone.

His pleas for help fell upon deaf ears as he tried to crawl away, but the enormous dog refused to let him go. He was *extremely* strong and had an unquenchable thirst for bitch-nigga blood.

In an instant, Charlie started seeing his life flash before his eyes as the tiger-striped killer persisted in trying to rip him apart. Just as he began to accept death, he saw six women, all toting AR-15s with 100-round monkey-nut drums. They were all amazingly gorgeous women, all of them thick like exotic dancers and rap music video vixens. Seeing them with the big guns had Charlie stuck between awestruck and terrified. When it came to bad bitches with guns... most men ran for the hills, scared shitless.

Out of the six of them, the one that caught Charlie's eye the most was a somewhat tall and thick caramel-skinned chick, with long golden dread locks. She was so beautiful that he, just for a moment, stopped feeling the pain of teeth in his flesh.

"Release!" he heard her yell.

Hearing the command, the dog stopped attacking Charlie. Obediently, the dog ran to the dread-head chick's side. Charlie looked up at her Asian-like face and saw her smirking at him, like a sexy devil.

One of the other women, a voluptuous Latina who also had rich creamy caramel colored skin, walked to where he laid, bloody and with bite marks all over him. Stopping just a foot away from him, the woman crouched down low, and looked down into his eyes, giving him the same devilish smile as the dread head chick.

"You *know* you fucked up, right?" she asked him.

Then from out of nowhere, a blunt object came and whacked him right in his face, knocking him clean out.

***

With Deuce standing obediently by her side, Bunz listened to the Russian beg and plead for his life, after he was repeatedly smacked back to consciousness. The way he was crying and begging made her laugh.

Why do so many punk-ass niggas that call themselves killers turn to straight bitches when the girls got the guns, she thought to herself, as Yessinia and G-Baby stood in front of Charlie.

"Please don't kill me! It was all Bruno, he is the one that decided to take the girls," Charlie blubbered turning into a damn snitch.

"And like a follower, you stuck with him, huh?" Yessy asked the Russian, with narrowed eyes.

Charlie nodded his head, "Y-Yes. I... we have the money to have just purchased it from you, but he wanted to live dangerously."

Yessy chuckled. "Mission accomplished, *mamabicho*," she told him, calling him a dick sucker in Spanish.

Charlie was grabbed up by the statuesque Amazon tall butter pecan-brown skinned woman, her frosty Arctic Blue eyes filled with anger and hatred. Assisting her was the ridiculously thick golden-brown skinned chick with her hair dyed platinum-blonde and cut low on the right side of her head.

"Wait!" Charlie continued, "Look! All you must do is kill him! If you do, I will take over this company, and we can be partners! I can send a lot of business your way! Please!"

Ignoring him, Yessy turned his attention to Bunz.

"You see the type of shit we deal with when it comes to these snake-ass bitches? Muhfuckas wanna' snatch up my girls for a lil' bit of coke, then cry like bitches when a bunch of girls get at them."

Bunz nodded her head. "Tell me about it. Free food for my dog, though," she replied, looking at Charlie with an evil smirk.

Yessy looked back at where Michelle and Gloria had gotten Victoria and Simone untied from the chairs. They came to join the others then, having no intention of leaving until they go to see the Russian die.

Yessy looked back at the Russian and spoke. "*He who informs against his friends to get a share of their property, the eyes of his children will fall*," she said to him. "My husband did some time in the joint. We talked every day and at some point, he picked up the Bible and started reading it. He told me about this verse one night, and I'm like, no *effing* way does it advise against snitching in the bitch. So, he had me look it up, and sure enough, right in the book of *Job, Chapter 17: Verse 5*, in the *Gideon* version, I saw it. Do you know what this means for you?"

Trembling in fear, Charlie shook his head.

"It means, snitches get eaten by big ass XXL Bullies," Yessy told him, then Bunz shouted the command to Deuce, releasing him to do what he did best.

"No! No! Please, do not kill me! I didn't want this, it was Bruno!" Charlie sobbed.

"Don't worry. I will take care of him, too," Yessy assured him as Charlie was taken back to the ground and mauled.

The ladies all stood there and watched the Russian be ripped apart, chunk of flesh by chunk of flesh. Deuce delivered the death bite when he caught Charlie's throat and ripped the man's Adam's apple right out like his neck was made of paper. The dog chomped and chewed it, then swallowed.

"I should have brought my dogs to join in," Yessy said, thinking of her and her man's killer German Rottweiler and Red Nose Pit Bull.

"Me, too. Fendi would've *loved* to show off how good she is at killin' pussy muthafuckas like him," added G-Baby, speaking of her trained-to-kill Cane Corso.

"So would Demon and Diamond," chimed in the Dominican belle Michelle of her own Cane Corsos, whom were the mother and father of G-Baby's dog.

The 6'0 tall Puerto Rican-Colombian stallion ChaCha chuckled. "Y'alls dogs *still* ain't got on my baby Pablo, yo," she boasted in her thick New York accent.

"Well, your fucking dog is the size of a horse, *cabrona*," Yessy shot back, which made them all laugh.

"I'ma get a lion so y'all can't say shit about whose dog is the shit," the bodacious platinum-blonde Dominicana Evelyn said, as she hooked an arm around her milk-chocolate complexioned Dominicana lesbian lover Gloria.

"Womp womp! Fuck Simba," Yessy teased her. "Okay, ladies!" she then said to them all. "Let us go and see how silly the other guy looks now that he got caught, thinking he was going to get away," Yessy said. "¡Vamos, bitches!"

Chapter 16

Holding his Mossberg pump, Macho stood with his brother. They were joined by their two younger cousins Javier, Xavier, and their older cousin Danny. The men stood posted next to Macho's old Peterbilt, waiting for their escapee to be brought before them.

Just minutes ago, they had all heard the blood-curdling screams of a man, that lasted almost a minute long before they just... stopped. Macho knew his woman was handling business inside. He waited for his longtime friend Eric to appear with the top dog Russian.

Just then, coming around the side of the building, Macho and his people saw the Russian hit-squad boss with Eric behind him keeping his the sawed-off 10-gauge that he was gripping pointed at the back of Bruno's head. Trotting alongside of him was his big female XXL Bully.

Bruno was limping and whimpering with his nose bleeding and eye swollen. With one hand reached back, he held onto his ass. Mach saw that LaLa and saw blood was smeared around her snout. He and the others busted out laughing.

"Daaaaayuuuum, cutty! Yo' dog took a bite out of bitch, huh?" Macho clowned.

Eric chuckled as he kicked the back of Bruno's right knee in, making him fall to his knees on the ground.

"Yeah. I'm surprised, though. She never used to like the taste of bitch," Eric told him, right before he bashed Bruno in the back of his head with the butt of his shotgun.

Bruno yelped in pain as he flew face first to the ground and laid there, dazed. Macho went and crouched down next to him. He reached down and grabbed Bruno by a lock of hair and yanked his head up, making him look up into his eyes.

"You know you fucked up, right?" he told him, with a goofy smile.

Bruno sneered at her, attempting to intimidate Macho. "Do you know who I am? My cousin is Ivan Radanovich! The most feared man in all of Russia! If I do not walk out of here alive, he will come, and he will kill you all!"

Macho shook his head at him. "Do you *really* think empty threats will do *anything* for you at this moment, *mamaguevo?*" he insulted him in Spanish.

Right then, Eric saw his woman and Deuce exit the building, along with Macho's ladies, Yessy and G-Baby, Javi's wife Michelle and his baby sister Evelyn, Danny's wife ChaCha, with Simone and Victoria safe and sound.

Looking back at Bruno, despite him having a hard face, Macho could tell he was shook. As the others got to where they were, Macho stood back up. Yessy and G-Baby both walked up to their man. Bunz walked up to hers. Michelle went to her husband and ChaCha went to hers.

"Next time, I'm bringin' *my* ladies," Xavier said, feeling a little left out without his wife and his two ride or die baby mommas.

Eric put an arm around Bunz and kissed her cheek. He leaned close to her ear and whispered something to her that made her giggle.

Macho looked down at the Russian and smirked, "Your man is pieces of protein inside my homeboy's dog's stomach. *You*, on the other hand, are a sick bastard. You are going to suffer *way* worse than ya mans did but first, my two friends that were only trying to do their job, are going to have their way with you."

Danny and Tool grabbed Bruno. Immediately, the Russian's tough act cracked. He started begging for mercy. *"Wait! Wait! I can pay you for my freedom! Please, whatever you want!"* he shouted as the two absurdly strong men lifted him from the ground and held him in place.

Macho stepped up to Bruno, looking down into his terror-stricken eyes. "Only God forgives, my man. I, on the other hand, do *not*," he said, then he busted out laughing at himself. "I have *always* wanted to say that to someone."

G-Baby pulled out a hypodermic needle from her sweatpants pocket and took the cap off. The syringe was filled with *night-night* juice. Bruno tried to buck and kick free, but he was no match in strength for Danny and Tool.

G-Baby jabbed the needle into Bruno's neck. Seconds after she pushed the plunger down, injecting him with the strong knock-out sedative. Withing seconds Bruno started feeling the effects and fell out like a broken lightbulb.

"Time to go, people," Macho said, then he and Tool tossed the Russian up over the side of the dump trailer.

Eric, Bunz, LaLa and Deuce got up into the old Peterbilt with Yessy, G-Baby, Simone and Victoria. ChaCha and Danny hopped into Danny's 2003 matte-gray Lamborghini Reventón, while Javi, his wife, Xavier, their sister, and her girlfriend hopped into Evelyn's new all-black Cadillac Escalade.

As they all pulled off Macho and Tool ran over to where Simone's Freightliner Classic XL and Victoria's Peterbilt 389 were. The two hopped up inside the heavy-hauler rigs and hurried out of the quarry with the others.

Sitting in the luxurious box-shaped sleeper that the old Peterbilt had, Eric and Bunz sat with the two freed drivers. The sounds of ringing from someone making a call came through the speakers just then. Eric and Bunz heard a man answer the call.

"How much Aspirin am I gonna need on this one?" asked the guy, as his voice came out of the speakers.

Yessy chuckled. "A lot; don't worry, officer. I'll buy 'em for you," she told the man.

The cop on the other line grumbled. "Great. Thanks a lot," he said sarcastically, then the call was ended.

***

A few weeks after assisting the Valdez family with getting their people back and Eric and Bunz had a special appointment to get to. They were both giddy with excitement, wondering the whole way from their house to their destination, what they were going to learn.

They arrived at the doctor's office, and he parked the brand new silver and black 2-tone *Brabus* 700 edition Rolls-Royce Ghost that he had bought for his woman just days ago near the front and went around to help her out.

"Goddamn, baby," Eric said, as Bunz stepped out, looking good in the form-fitting Fendi dress she had on.

It was light brown with dark brown *F*s monogrammed all over it. The long black sleeves it had were see-through and looked like the black pantyhose that she slid her shapely bottom half into. Down on her feet, despite her big belly, Bunz wore light brown pointed-toe Fendi pumps, with 5-inch heels.

The pricey dress fit her body so perfectly. It allowed her *double-baby* bump to be on full display, along with her wider-than-normal hips, and her even *fatter* ass.

She recently had her dreads dyed a rich golden color and the color complimented her flawless skin tone. In simple sweats and sneakers, Eric was blown away by her every day, but in such a sexy ensemble, he *yearned* for her in the worst way.

"Bunz, there is no female in the world that is as bad as you, baby," Eric told her, taking a second to appreciate how truly stunning his woman was.

Bunz started grinning, feeling all shy suddenly.

"Aww. Not one?" she asked him, putting her arms around his waist.

"Nope. I officially do not give a fuck about Nia Long anymore, so you are number one, my queen."

Bunz busted out laughing. "Good. Because she was gon' get knocked the fuck out if I ever met her. Now let's go inside and see what we gon' be chasin' around like maniacs in a few more months."

***

"Well would 'ya look at that! Somebody's gonna have two little one's months from now!" the ultrasound technician told Bunz and Eric, as she showed them the fetuses of twins on the screen, growing inside of Bunz's large belly.

Bunz was ecstatic to see she was bringing into the world *two* children by the man she loved more than life itself.

"Looks like we have one little girl and a little boy!" the tech continued.

"Wow! A momma's boy, and a daddy's girl! I love it!" Eric exclaimed.

Bunz was in tears from how happy she was, and he kissed the hand that he had been holding the entire time.

"Thank you so much, baby. You make me so happy," he told her, as tears of joy welled up in his own eyes.

His words were like sweet love music to her ears.

"It's you and me, E," she told him, then added, "forever, baby."

"Forever, baby," he nodded, then raised their clasped hands up, looking at the matching finger tattoos they'd gotten.

Bunz's finger said, *Forever His Queen*, while Eric's said, *Forever Her King*; over their hearts, they both had tatted, *M&E 4EVER*.

"Congratulations to you two," the ultrasound tech said, with a warm smile, "I can tell you both are going to be the greatest parents. I meet a lot of couple in this field of work, but the chemistry you two have is rare. You two were literally made for each other. That is God's work."

Smiling at each other, Bunz and Eric agreed wholeheartedly with the nurse.

"We most definitely are," Eric said.

"Yes indeed," Bunz then said.

***

Holding her hand, Eric escorted his future wife out of the doctor's office to the parking lot. He got her seated in the passenger's seat, hopped in behind the wheel, and started the engine.

Bunz's iPhone rang as he put it into drive. She saw a random number was calling.

"Hello?"

"Hi, my name is Clarissa Mulinaro. May I speak with Ms. Duque?"

"This is she."

"Hi, Ms. Duque. I'm calling about your desire to find a building adequate for your assisted-living program. Are you still interested in one?"

"Yes, I am. You have one for sale?" Bunz asked, as Eric cruised along Madison Avenue, towards downtown.

"I do, and it's a beautiful building. It's located across from Six Flags: Great America, in the Gurnee area. Are you familiar with it?"

"Yes. When can I see it?"

"Well, I'm actually able to show it to you now, if you'd like?"

"I can be there in an hour."

"Great! See you then, Ms. Duque!"

The call ended. Bunz told Eric about the call. He smiled and nodded his head.

"To Gurnee then," he said, and headed towards the E-Way.

***

An hour later, after passing up the American Eagle rollercoaster at the side of 94 in Gurnee, Eric got off at Grand Avenue. Bunz smiled when she saw the three restaurants there. It brought her back to the time when she rolled the dice and made the biggest gamble when she chose to return to him.

Travelling east on Grand, Eric reached where the entrance to the big amusement park was. He got into the left-turn lane was and waited for the light to turn green. They both looked to their left and saw the houses on one side. Further to their left, they both saw the big apartment building there, with a red and white brick façade.

The light turned green. Eric made the turn and pulled into the lot. Only a van and a Mercedes SUV were parked in front. He parked next to the GL63 AMG, killed the engine, and got out to go help his pregnant fiancée out.

Walking towards the entrance to the building together, the glass front door opened and out came a tall blonde woman, wearing a khaki-colored skirt suit with yellow pumps on her feet, carrying a leather briefcase in her hand.

"Hello! You must be Ms. Duque! Oh, my word! Look at that belly!" she said to Bunz, smiling excitedly at the big Fendi baby-bump.

Bunz chuckled, appreciating the woman's enthusiasm. "Yes. This is my fiancé Eric Bounds," Bunz told her.

The woman smiled and shook his hand. "How do you do? I am Clarissa Mulinaro. I'd like to thank you both for coming out on such short notice. I came across your ad searching for a commercial building and gave the number listed a call right away. Shall we go in and see what you'd be getting if you purchased this prime location?"

"Lead the way," Bunz told her.

Clarissa held the door and entered behind them. Bunz felt the cold and refreshing air conditioning inside, which told her that the maintenance on the building was likely up to par. Eric saw fresh paint and new flooring. He already liked what he saw.

"I hope you guys are ready for this," Clarissa said, as she beckoned them to where an elevator was, "your lives are about to change forever!"

Following her, Bunz chuckled. "From purchasing this building?" she asked, as Clarissa hit a button to call down the elevator.

The button for the 1st floor lit up. The sound of the elevator car descending came. As it dinged from reaching the lobby floor, Clarissa turned to them, with a smile that was no longer warm and friendly, but evil and twisted.

"Nope," she said, as the doors opened. "From learning a really hard and painful lesson about fucking with the *wrong* people."

Eric and Bunz saw four big men inside the elevator, with assault rifles. Eric's eyes went wide with shock, when he saw none other than Anastasia in front of them, holding a pistol in her hand.

Bunz gasped when she saw the woman raise her gun up and point it at Eric, as she and the men behind her stepped out of the elevator. She and Eric were then surrounded by the two ladies and the men.

"What the fuck is this?!" Bunz demanded to know with her hand trying to get into her Fendi handbag, as Eric stared Anastasia down.

CLICK CLACK

157

Clarissa had pulled her own pistol out from her briefcase and pointed it at Bunz's head.

One of the men took Bunz's bag away from her and pulled the gun she had in it out, tucking it into his own waistline.

"I'll tell you what's going on, bitch," Anastasia spoke, looking at Eric with pure hatred. "First off, I fucked your man right before I sent him to kill my back-stabbing husband. He was skimming me of the inheritance that my father left for me."

Bunz's jaw dropped when she heard that the man she was devoted to had piped another bitch down.

"Eric! What the fuck is she talking about?" she snapped at him.

"It's quite simple, stupid. I sucked his cock then he fucked me. But that's beside the point; I just wanted you to feel the agonizing pain of havin' love taken from you, before I take your love from you," she told Bunz.

"What the fuck do you want?! Who are you?!" Bunz asked.

"Your man thinks my name is Anastasia, but it's not." She paused and looked at Bunz finally. "My name is Paulina Paulmatti… you killed my father and my mother, then you stole the diamonds he'd been saving to give to *me*!"

Eric and Bunz both felt their hearts drop. Paulina saw the fear in their eyes. She chuckled to herself as did Clarissa.

"Yeah. You fucked up and I see that it's sinking in now," she said, before she took the gun from pointing at Eric, to pointing it at Bunz's belly.

"NO!" Bunz shrieked.

Eric dove in front of her right as Paula squeezed the trigger.

Bunz screamed at the tops of her lungs when her fiancé hit the floor after four shots hit him in his chest. He fell to the floor, face down, not moving.

"Nooo! Eric, baby! Eric!" Bunz cried, trying to grab for him, but held back by two of the men.

BOC! BOC! BOC! BOC! BOC!

Paula popped Eric in his back four more times. She smirked to herself, looking at the motionless hit man on the floor.

Bunz tried like held to rip free from the grasp of the two men, but they were too strong, and she wasn't strong enough.

"Enough, bitch! Silence!" Paula pointed her gun right at Bunz's face. Bunz stopped fighting as fear from a bullet in the face made her freeze. "This is what's going to happen; you are coming with me, and you are going to give me my goddamned diamonds, or…" she said pausing again as she stepped closer to Bunz, putting the barrel of her gun right on Bunz's stomach. "I am going to cut your fucking stomach open with rusty scissors, and I will make you watch me put whatever comes out in a fucking microwave!"

Bunz screamed and cried and begged as a bag was put over her head and tied. She felt herself being lifted off of the ground, then stabbed in the neck by something very small and sharp.

Seconds later, as she felt herself being carried away, everything went dark…

TO BE CONTINUED…

Lock Down Publications and Ca$h Presents
Assisted Publishing Packages

Due to an increase in the price of services we have increased our prices. The prices below reflect the price increase as of 11/1/24.

BASIC PACKAGE $699 Editing Cover Design Formatting	UPGRADED PACKAGE $1000 Typing Editing Cover Design Formatting Upload eBooks to Amazon Upload Paperback to Amazon
ADVANCE PACKAGE $1,400 Typing Editing (line editing/content) Cover Design Formatting Copyright Registration Proofreading Upload eBooks to Amazon Upload Paperback to Amazon	LDP SUPREME PACKAGE $1,700 Typing Editing (line editing/content) Cover Design Formatting Copyright Registration Proofreading Set up Amazon Account Upload eBooks to Amazon Upload Paperback to Amazon Advertise on LDP's Amazon and Facebook Page

***Other services available upon request.
Additional charges may apply

Lock Down Publications
P.O. Box 944
Stockbridge, GA 30281-9998
Phone: 470 303-9761
Email: lockdownpublications@gmail.com

Submission Guideline

Submit the first three chapters of your completed manuscript to ldpsubmissions@gmail.com. In the subject line add **Your Book's Title**. The manuscript must be in a Word Doc file and sent as an attachment. Document should be in Times New Roman, double spaced, and in size 12 font. Also, provide your synopsis and full contact information. If sending multiple submissions, they must each be in a separate email.

Have a story but no way to send it electronically? You can still submit to LDP/Ca$h Presents. Send in the first three chapters, written or typed, of your completed manuscript to:

LDP: Submissions Dept
P.O. Box 944
Stockbridge, GA 30281-9998

DO NOT send original manuscript. Must be a duplicate.
Provide your synopsis and a cover letter containing your full contact information.

Thanks for considering LDP and Ca$h Presents.

NEW RELEASES

BLOODLINE OF A SAVAGE 1,2&3
THESE VICIOUS STREETS 1,2&3
RELENTLESS GOON
RELENTLESS GOON 2
BY PRINCE A. TAUHID

THE BUTTERFLY MAFIA 1-3
BY FUMIYA PAYNE

A THUG'S STREET PRINCESS 1,2&3
BY MEESHA

CITY OF SMOKE 1& 2
BY MOLOTTI

STEPPERS 1,2&3
THE REAL BADDIES OF CHI-RAQ
BY KING RIO

THE LANE 1&2
BY KEN-KEN SPENCE

THUG OF SPADES 1,2&3
LOVE IN THE TRENCHES 2
CORNER BOY CHRONICLES
BY COREY ROBINSON

TIL DEATH 3
BY ARYANNA

THE BIRTH OF A GANGSTER 4
BY DELMONT PLAYER

PROBLEM SOLVED

PRODUCT OF THE STREETS 1&2
BY DEMOND "MONEY" ANDERSON

NO TIME FOR ERROR
BY KEESE

MONEY HUNGRY DEMONS 1,2&3
BY TRANAY ADAMS

HUNGRY FOR MONEY 1&2
BY SLIMBOS

A THUGGISH PASSION
KILLAZ ON STANDBY 1&2
LAND OF DA HOOLIGANZ 1,2&3
FRESH OFF DA PORCH
BY IRA B.

COUNTDOWN OF A KILLA 1&2
GUNS DOWN, BOTTOMS UP 1&2
SEX, MURDA AND GOD
BY LO-LIFE

THE LEVEL UP 1&2
BY LUXURY KING

FO'EVA ROLLIN' 1&2
BY ASSA RAYMOND BAKER

HUB CITY MENACE 1&2
BY J. WHITE

KILLA CREW
DYING FOR LIKES
BY ARYANNA

CHRISTOPHER "DIESEL" HORNEZES

IF YOU CROSS ME ONCE 6
ANGEL 5
By Anthony Fields

IMMA DIE BOUT MINE 5
By Aryanna

A THUGS STREET PRINCESS 3
EMBRACING THE LOVE OF A BOSS
By Meesha

PRODUCT OF THE STREETS 3
By Demond Money Anderson

STANDING ON HER BUSINESS
BY DG SANTANA

GET IT IN SLUGS 1&2
B. STALLS

CORNER BOYS 2
By Corey Robinson

THE MURDER QUEENS 6&7
By Michael Gallon

CITY OF SMOKE 3
By Molotti

CONFESSIONS OF A DOPEBOY
By Nicholas Lock

TENDER
BY KHUFU

PROBLEM SOLVED

THA TAKEOVER
By Keith Chandler

BETRAYAL OF A G 2
By Ray Vinci

CRIME BOSS 4
By Playa Ray

Coming Soon from Lock Down Publications/Ca$h Presents

RAN OFF ON THE PLUG 2 by **PAPER BOI RARI**
STREET REDEMPTION by **TONY DANIELS**
SAVAGE FAMILY EMPIRE by **PRINCE TAUHID**
BAD BITCHES WIT' GUNZ by **DIESEL**
THE SINGLE LADIES by **DIESEL**
COKE BY THE TRUCKLOAD by **DIESEL**
PROBLEM SOLVED by **DIESEL**
TIPPIN' THE SCALES by **DIESEL**
OPPS CRY TOO by **SAYNOMORE**
A GANGSTA'S KARMA by **FLAME**

AVAILABLE NOW

RESTRAINING ORDER 1 & 2
By **CA$H & Coffee**

LOVE KNOWS NO BOUNDARIES 1-3
By **Coffee**

RAISED AS A GOON I, II, III & IV
BRED BY THE SLUMS I, II, III
BLAST FOR ME I & II
ROTTEN TO THE CORE I II III
A BRONX TALE I, II, III
DUFFLE BAG CARTEL I II III IV V VI
HEARTLESS GOON I II III IV V
A SAVAGE DOPEBOY I II
DRUG LORDS I II III
CUTTHROAT MAFIA I II
KING OF THE TRENCHES
By **Ghost**

LAY IT DOWN I & II
LAST OF A DYING BREED I II
BLOOD STAINS OF A SHOTTA I & II III
By **Jamaica**

LOYAL TO THE GAME I II III
LIFE OF SIN I, II III
By **TJ & Jelissa**

IF LOVING HIM IS WRONG…I & II
LOVE ME EVEN WHEN IT HURTS I II III
By **Jelissa**

CHRISTOPHER "DIESEL" HORNEZES

PUSH IT TO THE LIMIT
By **Bre' Hayes**

BLOODY COMMAS I & II
SKI MASK CARTEL I, II & III
KING OF NEW YORK I II, III IV V
RISE TO POWER I II III
COKE KINGS I II III IV V
BORN HEARTLESS I II III IV
KING OF THE TRAP I II
By **T.J. Edwards**

WHEN THE STREETS CLAP BACK I & II III
THE HEART OF A SAVAGE I II III IV
MONEY MAFIA I II
LOYAL TO THE SOIL I II III
By **Jibril Williams**

A DISTINGUISHED THUG STOLE MY HEART I - III
LOVE SHOULDN'T HURT I II III IV
RENEGADE BOYS 1-4
PAID IN KARMA 1-3
SAVAGE STORMS 1-3
AN UNFORESEEN LOVE 1-3
BABY, I'M WINTERTIME COLD 1-3
A THUG'S STREET PRINCESS 1&2
By **Meesha**

CUM FOR ME 1-8
An LDP Erotica Collaboration

BLOOD OF A BOSS 1-5
SHADOWS OF THE GAME
TRAP BASTARD
By **Askari**

168

PROBLEM SOLVED

A GANGSTER'S CODE 1-3
A GANGSTER'S SYN 1-3
THE SAVAGE LIFE 1-3
CHAINED TO THE STREETS 1-3
BLOOD ON THE MONEY 1-3
A GANGSTA'S PAIN 1-3
BEAUTIFUL LIES AND UGLY TRUTHS
CHURCH IN THESE STREETS
By **J-Blunt**

THE STREETS BLEED MURDER 1-3
THE HEART OF A GANGSTA 1-3
By **Jerry Jackson**

WHEN A GOOD GIRL GOES BAD
By **Adrienne**

THE COST OF LOYALTY 1-3
By **Kweli**

BRIDE OF A HUSTLA 1-3
THE FETTI GIRLS 1-3
CORRUPTED BY A GANGSTA 1-4
BLINDED BY HIS LOVE
THE PRICE YOU PAY FOR LOVE 1-3
DOPE GIRL MAGIC 1-3
By **Destiny Skai**

A KINGPIN'S AMBITION
A KINGPIN'S AMBITION II
I MURDER FOR THE DOUGH
By **Ambitious**

A DOPEBOY'S PRAYER
By **Eddie "Wolf" Lee**

CHRISTOPHER "DIESEL" HORNEZES

TRUE SAVAGE 1-7
DOPE BOY MAGIC 1-3
MIDNIGHT CARTEL 1-3
CITY OF KINGZ 1&2
NIGHTMARE ON SILENT AVE
THE PLUG OF LIL MEXICO 1&2
CLASSIC CITY
By **Chris Green**

LOVE & CHASIN' PAPER
By **Qay Crockett**

THE KING CARTEL 1-3
By **Frank Gresham**

THESE NIGGAS AIN'T LOYAL 1-3
By **Nikki Tee**

GANGSTA SHYT 1-3
By **CATO**

THE ULTIMATE BETRAYAL
By **Phoenix**

BOSS'N UP 1-3
By **Royal Nicole**

I LOVE YOU TO DEATH
By **Destiny J**

BROOKLYN HUSTLAZ
By **Boogsy Morina**

GANGSTA CITY
By **Teddy Duke**

PROBLEM SOLVED

TO DIE IN VAIN
SINS OF A HUSTLA
By **ASAD**

I RIDE FOR MY HITTA
I STILL RIDE FOR MY HITTA
By **Misty Holt**

A GANGSTER'S REVENGE 1-4
THE BOSS MAN'S DAUGHTERS 1-5
A SAVAGE LOVE 1&2
BAE BELONGS TO ME 1&2
A HUSTLER'S DECEIT 1-3
WHAT BAD BITCHES DO 1-3
SOUL OF A MONSTER 1-3
KILL ZONE
A DOPE BOY'S QUEEN 1-3
TIL DEATH 1-3
IMMA DIE BOUT MINE 1-5
By **Aryanna**

BROOKLYN ON LOCK 1 & 2
By **Sonovia**

A DRUG KING AND HIS DIAMOND 1-3
A DOPEMAN'S RICHES
HER MAN, MINE'S TOO 1&2
CASH MONEY HO'S
THE WIFEY I USED TO BE 1&2
PRETTY GIRLS DO NASTY THINGS
By **Nicole Goosby**

THE STREETS ARE CALLING
By **Duquie Wilson**

LIPSTICK KILLAH 1-3
CRIME OF PASSION 1-3
FRIEND OR FOE 1-3
By **Mimi**

TRAPHOUSE KING 1-3
KINGPIN KILLAZ 1-3
STREET KINGS 1&2
PAID IN BLOOD 1&2
CARTEL KILLAZ 1-3
DOPE GODS 1&2
By **Hood Rich**

STEADY MOBBN' 1-3
THE STREETS STAINED MY SOUL 1-3
By **Marcellus Allen**

WHO SHOT YA 1-3
SON OF A DOPE FIEND 1-4
HEAVEN GOT A GHETTO 1&2
SKI MASK MONEY 1&2
By **Renta**

GORILLAZ IN THE BAY 1-4
TEARS OF A GANGSTA 1/&2
3X KRAZY 1&2
STRAIGHT BEAST MODE 1&2
By **DE'KARI**

TRIGGADALE 1-3
MURDA WAS THE CASE 1-3
By **Elijah R. Freeman**

MARRIED TO A BOSS 1-3
By **Destiny Skai & Chris Green**

PROBLEM SOLVED

SLAUGHTER GANG 1-3
RUTHLESS HEART 1-3
By **Willie Slaughter**

GOD BLESS THE TRAPPERS 1-3
THESE SCANDALOUS STREETS 1-3
FEAR MY GANGSTA 1-5
THESE STREETS DON'T LOVE NOBODY 1-2
BURY ME A G 1-5
A GANGSTA'S EMPIRE 1-4
THE DOPEMAN'S BODYGAURD 1&2
THE REALEST KILLAZ 1-3
THE LAST OF THE OGS 1-3
By **Tranay Adams**

KINGZ OF THE GAME 1-7
CRIME BOSS 1-4
By **Playa Ray**

FUK SHYT
By **Blakk Diamond**

DON'T F#CK WITH MY HEART 1&2
By **Linnea**

ADDICTED TO THE DRAMA 1-3
IN THE ARM OF HIS BOSS
By **Jamila**

LOYALTY AIN'T PROMISED 1&2
By **Keith Williams**

FOREVER GANGSTA 1&2
GLOCKS ON SATIN SHEETS 1&2
By **Adrian Dulan**

CHRISTOPHER "DIESEL" HORNEZES

YAYO 1-4
A SHOOTER'S AMBITION 1&2
BRED IN THE GAME
By **S. Allen**

TRAP GOD 1-3
RICH $AVAGE 1-3
MONEY IN THE GRAVE 1-3
CARTEL MONEY
By **Martell Troublesome Bolden**

TOE TAGZ 1-4
LEVELS TO THIS SHYT 1&2
IT'S JUST ME AND YOU
By **Ah'Million**

KINGPIN DREAMS 1-3
RAN OFF ON DA PLUG
By **Paper Boi Rari**

THE STREETS MADE ME 1-3
By **Larry D. Wright**

CONFESSIONS OF A GANGSTA 1-4
CONFESSIONS OF A JACKBOY 1-3
CONFESSIONS OF A HITMAN
By **Nicholas Lock**

I'M NOTHING WITHOUT HIS LOVE
SINS OF A THUG
TO THE THUG I LOVED BEFORE
A GANGSTA SAVED XMAS
IN A HUSTLER I TRUST
By **Monet Dragun**

PROBLEM SOLVED

QUIET MONEY 1-3
THUG LIFE 1-3
EXTENDED CLIP 1&2
A GANGSTA'S PARADISE
By **Trai'Quan**

CAUGHT UP IN THE LIFE 1-3
THE STREETS NEVER LET GO 1-3
By **Robert Baptiste**

NEW TO THE GAME 1-3
MONEY, MURDER & MEMORIES 1-3
By **Malik D. Rice**

THE LIFE OF A HOOD STAR
By **Ca$h & Rashia Wilson**

THE STREETS WILL NEVER CLOSE 1-4
By **K'ajji**

LIFE OF A SAVAGE 1-4
A GANGSTA'S QUR'AN 1-4
MURDA SEASON 1-3
GANGLAND CARTEL 1-3
CHI'RAQ GANGSTAS 1-4
KILLERS ON ELM STREET 1-3
JACK BOYZ N DA BRONX 1-3
A DOPEBOY'S DREAM 1-3
JACK BOYS VS DOPE BOYS 1-3
COKE GIRLZ
COKE BOYS
SOSA GANG 1&2
BRONX SAVAGES
BODYMORE KINGPINS
BLOOD OF A GOON
By **Romell Tukes**

CHRISTOPHER "DIESEL" HORNEZES

CREAM 2-3
THE STREETS WILL TALK
By **Yolanda Moore**

CONCRETE KILLA 1-3
VICIOUS LOYALTY 1-3
By **Kingpen**

THE ULTIMATE SACRIFICE 1-6
KHADIFI
IF YOU CROSS ME ONCE 1-5
ANGEL 1-4
IN THE BLINK OF AN EYE
By **Anthony Fields**

NIGHTMARES OF A HUSTLA 1-3
BLOOD AND GAMES 1&2
By **King Dream**

HARD AND RUTHLESS 1&2
MOB TOWN 251
THE BILLIONAIRE BENTLEYS 1-3
REAL G'S MOVE IN SILENCE
By **Von Diesel**

MOB TIES 1-7
SOUL OF A HUSTLER, HEART OF A KILLER 1-3
GORILLAZ IN THE TRENCHES
By **SayNoMore**

BODYMORE MURDERLAND 1-3
THE BIRTH OF A GANGSTER 1-4
By **Delmont Player**

FOR THE LOVE OF A BOSS 1&2
By **C. D. Blue**

PROBLEM SOLVED

KILLA KOUNTY 1-5
By **Khufu**

MOBBED UP 1-4
THE BRICK MAN 1-5
THE COCAINE PRINCESS 1-10
STEPPERS 1-3
SUPER GREMLIN 1-4
By **King Rio**

MONEY GAME 1&2
By **Smoove Dolla**

A GANGSTA'S KARMA 1-4
By **FLAME**

KING OF THE TRENCHES 1-3
By **GHOST & TRANAY ADAMS**

QUEEN OF THE ZOO 1&2
By **Black Migo**

GRIMEY WAYS 1-3
BETRAYAL OF A G
By **Ray Vinci**

XMAS WITH AN ATL SHOOTER
By **Ca$h & Destiny Skai**

KING KILLA 1&2
By **Vincent "Vitto" Holloway**

BETRAYAL OF A THUG 1&2
By **Fre$h**

CHRISTOPHER "DIESEL" HORNEZES

THE MURDER QUEENS 1-6
By **Michael Gallon**

FOR THE LOVE OF BLOOD 1-4
By **Jamel Mitchell**

HOOD CONSIGLIERE 1&2
NO TIME FOR ERROR
By **Keese**

PROTÉGÉ OF A LEGEND 1&2
LOVE IN THE TRENCHES 1&2
By **Corey Robinson**

THE PLUG'S RUTHLESS DAUGHTER 1&2
By **Tony Daniels**

BORN IN THE GRAVE 1-3
CRIME PAYS 1&2
By **Self Made Tay**

MOAN IN MY MOUTH
By **XTASY**

TORN BETWEEN A GANGSTER AND A
GENTLEMAN
By **J-BLUNT & Miss Kim**

HERE TODAY GONE TOMORROW 1&2
By **Fly Rock**

PILLOW PRINCESS
By **S. Hawkins**

SANCTIFIED AND HORNY
by **XTASY**

PROBLEM SOLVED

WOMEN LIE MEN LIE 1-4
FIFTY SHADES OF SNOW 1-3
STACK BEFORE YOU SPLURGE
GIRLS FALL LIKE DOMINOES
NAÏVE TO THE STREETS
By **ROY MILLIGAN**

LOYALTY IS EVERYTHING 1-3
CITY OF SMOKE 1&2
By **Molotti**

THE BUTTERFLY MAFIA 1-4
SALUTE MY SAVAGERY 1&2
By **Fumiya Payne**

THE LANE 1&2
By **Ken-Ken Spence**

THE PUSSY TRAP 1-5
By **Nene Capri**

DIRTY DNA
By **Blaque**

BOOKS BY LDP'S CEO, CA$H

TRUST IN NO MAN
TRUST IN NO MAN 2
TRUST IN NO MAN 3
BONDED BY BLOOD
SHORTY GOT A THUG
THUGS CRY
THUGS CRY 2
THUGS CRY 3
TRUST NO BITCH
TRUST NO BITCH 2
TRUST NO BITCH 3
TIL MY CASKET DROPS
RESTRAINING ORDER
RESTRAINING ORDER 2
IN LOVE WITH A CONVICT
LIFE OF A HOOD STAR
XMAS WITH AN ATL SHOOTER

www.ingramcontent.com/pod-product-compliance
Lightning Source LLC
Chambersburg PA
CBHW071214260626
47162CB00004B/1297